PRAISE FOR RAYMIE NIGHTINGALE

A National Book Award Finalist

A *New York Times Book Review* Notable Book of the Year

"This triumphant and necessary book conjures the enchantments of childhood without shying away from the fraught realities."
— *The New York Times Book Review*

"Fast and fleet—a crystalline ode to childhood friendship that shines as brightly as anything DiCamillo has written."
— *The Chicago Tribune*

"Some readers may require tissues. . . . DiCamillo understands that children can handle the tough stuff in fiction—after all, they have to handle problems like divorce, grief, abuse, and poverty in real life. And a book like this can help."
— Time Magazine

"What a perfect plot setup: two friends competing for a common goal and a third dead-set on derailing it."
— *New York Journal of Books*

"Raymie's earnestness is impossible not to fall in love with. . . . Poignant."
— *Entertainment Weekly*

"A book to savor, to read and re-read. . . . DiCamillo's unique wry voice gives readers vivid images, dizzying ideas, humor, heart-wrenching emotions, and gorgeous, gorgeous language."
— *The Huffington Post*

"Quirky, heartfelt. . . . This coming-of-age story is a fairy tale for our times."
— *The Washington Post*

NOVELS BY KATE DiCAMILLO

Because of Winn-Dixie

The Tiger Rising

The Tale of Despereaux

The Miraculous Journey of Edward Tulane

The Magician's Elephant

Flora & Ulysses

Raymie Nightingale

Louisiana's Way Home

Beverly, Right Here

Raymie Nightingale

Kate DiCamillo

CANDLEWICK PRESS

Copyright © 2016 by Kate DiCamillo

First paperback edition 2018

Library of Congress Catalog Card Number 2015954528
ISBN 978-0-7636-8117-3 (hardcover)
ISBN 978-0-7636-9691-7 (paperback)

19 20 21 22 23 TRC 10 9 8 7 6 5

Printed in Eagan, MN, U.S.A.

This book was typeset in Joanna MT.

Candlewick Press
99 Dover Street
Somerville, Massachusetts 02144

visit us at www.candlewick.com

For my rancheros . . . thank you.

One

There were three of them, three girls.

They were standing side by side.

They were standing at attention.

And then the girl in the pink dress, the one who was standing right next to Raymie, let out a sob and said, "The more I think about it, the more terrified I am. I am too terrified to go on!"

The girl clutched her baton to her chest and dropped to her knees.

Raymie stared at her in wonder and admiration.

She herself often felt too terrified to go on, but she had never admitted it out loud.

The girl in the pink dress moaned and toppled over sideways.

Her eyes fluttered closed. She was silent. And then she opened her eyes very wide and shouted, "Archie, I'm sorry! I'm sorry I betrayed you!"

She closed her eyes again. Her mouth fell open.

Raymie had never seen or heard anything like it.

"I'm sorry," Raymie whispered. "I betrayed you."

For some reason, the words seemed worth repeating.

"Stop this nonsense immediately," said Ida Nee.

Ida Nee was the baton-twirling instructor. Even though she was old—over fifty at least— her hair was an extremely bright yellow. She wore white boots that came all the way up to her knees.

"I'm not kidding," said Ida Nee.

Raymie believed her.

Ida Nee didn't seem like much of a kidder.

The sun was way, way up in the sky, and the whole thing was like high noon in a Western. But it was not a Western; it was baton-twirling lessons at Ida Nee's house in Ida Nee's backyard.

It was the summer of 1975.

It was the fifth day of June.

And two days before, on the third day of June, Raymie Clarke's father had run away from home with a woman who was a dental hygienist.

Hey, diddle, diddle, the dish ran away with the spoon.

Those were the words that went through Raymie's head every time she thought about her father and the dental hygienist.

But she did not say the words out loud anymore because Raymie's mother was very upset, and talking about dishes and spoons running away together was not appropriate.

It was actually a great tragedy, what had happened.

That was what Raymie's mother said.

"This is a great tragedy," said Raymie's mother. "Quit reciting nursery rhymes."

It was a great tragedy because Raymie's father had disgraced himself.

It was also a great tragedy because Raymie was now fatherless.

The thought of that — the fact of it — that she, Raymie Clarke, was without a father, made a small, sharp pain shoot through Raymie's heart every time she considered it.

Sometimes the pain in her heart made her feel too terrified to go on. Sometimes it made her want to drop to her knees.

But then she would remember that she had a plan.

Two

"Get up," said Ida Nee to the girl in the pink dress.

"She fainted," said the other baton-twirling student, a girl named Beverly Tapinski, whose father was a cop.

Raymie knew the girl's name and what her father did because Beverly had made an announcement at the beginning of the lesson. She had stared straight ahead, not looking at anybody in particular, and said, "My name is Beverly Tapinski and my father is a cop, so I don't think that you should mess with me."

Raymie, for one, had no intention of messing with her.

"I've seen a lot of people faint," said Beverly now. "That's what happens when you're the daughter of a cop. You see everything. You see it all."

"Shut up, Tapinski," said Ida Nee.

The sun was very high in the sky.

It hadn't moved.

It seemed like someone had stuck it up there and then walked away and left it.

"I'm sorry," whispered Raymie. "I betrayed you."

Beverly Tapinski knelt down and put her hands on either side of the fainting girl's face.

"What do you think you're doing?" said Ida Nee.

The pine trees above them swayed back and forth. The lake, Lake Clara — where someone named Clara Wingtip had managed to drown herself a hundred years ago — gleamed and glittered.

The lake looked hungry.

Maybe it was hoping for another Clara Wingtip.

Raymie felt a wave of despair.

There wasn't time for people fainting. She had to learn how to twirl a baton and she had to learn fast, because if she learned how to twirl a baton, then she stood a good chance of becoming Little Miss Central Florida Tire.

And if she became Little Miss Central Florida Tire, her father would see her picture in the paper and come home.

That was Raymie's plan.

Three

The way that Raymie imagined her plan unfolding was that her father would be sitting in some restaurant, in whatever town he had run away to. He would be with Lee Ann Dickerson, the dental hygienist. They would be sitting together in a booth, and her father would be smoking a cigarette and drinking coffee, and Lee Ann would be doing something stupid and inappropriate, like maybe filing her nails (which you should never do in public). At some point, Raymie's father would put out his cigarette and open the paper and clear his throat and say, "Let's see what we can see here," and what he would see would be Raymie's picture.

He would see his daughter with a crown on her head and a bouquet of flowers in her arms and a sash across her chest that said LITTLE MISS CENTRAL FLORIDA TIRE 1975.

And Raymie's father, Jim Clarke of Clarke Family Insurance, would turn to Lee Ann and say, "I must return home immediately. Everything has changed. My daughter is now famous. She has been crowned Little Miss Central Florida Tire."

Lee Ann would stop filing her nails. She would gasp out loud in surprise and dismay (and also, maybe, in envy and admiration).

That's the way Raymie imagined it would happen.

Probably. Maybe. Hopefully.

But first she needed to learn how to twirl a baton.

Or so said Mrs. Sylvester.

Four

Mrs. Sylvester was the secretary at Clarke Family Insurance.

Mrs. Sylvester's voice was very high-pitched. She sounded like a little cartoon bird when she talked, and this made everything that she said seem ridiculous but also possible — both things at the same time.

When Raymie told Mrs. Sylvester that she was going to enter the Little Miss Central Florida Tire contest, Mrs. Sylvester had clapped her hands together and said, "What a wonderful idea. Have some candy corn."

Mrs. Sylvester kept an extremely large jar of candy corn on her desk at all times and in all seasons because she believed in feeding people.

She also believed in feeding swans. Every day on her lunch break, Mrs. Sylvester took a bag of swan food and went down to the pond by the hospital.

Mrs. Sylvester was very short, and the swans were tall and long-necked. When Mrs. Sylvester stood in the middle of them with her scarf on her head and the big bag of swan food in her arms, she looked like something out of a fairy tale.

Raymie wasn't sure which fairy tale.

Maybe it was a fairy tale that hadn't been told yet.

When Raymie asked Mrs. Sylvester what she thought about Jim Clarke leaving town with a dental hygienist, Mrs. Sylvester had said, "Well, dear, I have found that most things work out right in the end."

Did most things work out right in the end?
Raymie wasn't sure.

The idea seemed ridiculous (but also possible)
when Mrs. Sylvester said it in her tiny bird voice.

"If you intend to win the Little Miss Central
Florida Tire contest," said Mrs. Sylvester, "you
must learn how to twirl a baton. And the best person to teach you how to twirl a baton is Ida Nee.
She is a world champion."

Five

This explained what Raymie was doing in Ida Nee's backyard, under Ida Nee's pine trees.

She was learning how to twirl a baton.

Or that was what she was supposed to be doing.

But then the girl in the pink dress fainted, and the twirling lesson came to a screeching halt.

Ida Nee said, "This is ridiculous. No one faints in my classes. I don't believe in fainting."

Fainting didn't seem like the kind of thing that you needed to believe in (or not) in order for it to happen, but Ida Nee was a world-champion twirler and she probably knew what she was talking about.

"It is just nonsense," said Ida Nee. "I don't have time for nonsense."

This pronouncement was greeted with a small silence, and then Beverly Tapinski slapped the girl in the pink dress.

She slapped one cheek and then the other one.

"What in the world?" said Ida Nee.

"This is what you do for people who faint," said Beverly. "You slap them." She slapped the girl again. "Wake up!" she shouted.

The girl opened her eyes. "Uh-oh," she said. "Has the county home come? Is Marsha Jean here?"

"I don't know any Marsha Jean," said Beverly. "You fainted."

"Did I?" She blinked. "I have very swampy lungs."

"This lesson is over," said Ida Nee. "I'm not wasting my time with lollygaggers and malingerers. Or fainters."

"Good," said Beverly. "No one wants to learn how to twirl a stupid baton anyway."

Which was not true.

Raymie wanted to learn.

In fact, she needed to learn.

But it didn't seem like a good idea to disagree with Beverly.

Ida Nee marched away from them, down to the lake. She lifted her white-booted legs very high. You could tell that she was a world champion just by watching her march.

"Sit up," said Beverly to the fainting girl.

The girl sat up. She looked around her in wonder, as if she had been deposited on Ida Nee's property by mistake. She blinked. She put her hand on her head. "My brain feels light as a feather," she said.

"Duh," said Beverly. "That's because you fainted."

"I'm afraid that I wouldn't have made a very good Flying Elefante," said the girl.

There was a long silence.

"What's an elefante?" asked Raymie finally.

The girl blinked. Her blond hair shone white in the sun. "I'm an Elefante. My name is Louisiana Elefante. My parents were the Flying Elefantes. Haven't you heard of them?"

"No," said Beverly. "We haven't heard of them. You should try to stand up now."

Louisiana put her hand on her chest. She took a deep breath. She wheezed.

Beverly rolled her eyes. "Here," she said. She held out her hand. It was a grubby hand. The fingers were smudged, and the nails were dirty and chewed down. But in spite of its grubbiness, or maybe because of it, it was a very certain-looking hand.

Louisiana took hold of it, and Beverly pulled her to her feet.

"Oh, my goodness," said Louisiana. "I'm just all filled up with feathers and regrets. And fears. I have a lot of fears."

She stood there staring at both of them. Her eyes were dark. They were brown. No, they were black, and they were set very deep in her face. She blinked. "I've got a question for you," she said. "Have you ever in your life come to realize that everything, absolutely everything, depends on you?"

Raymie didn't even have to think about the answer to this question. "Yes," she said.

"Duh," said Beverly.

"It's terrifying, isn't it?" said Louisiana.

The three of them stood there looking at one another.

Raymie felt something expanding inside of her. It felt like a gigantic tent billowing out.

This, Raymie knew, was her soul.

Mrs. Borkowski, who lived across the street from Raymie and who was very, very old, said that most people wasted their souls.

"How do they waste them?" Raymie had asked.

"They let them shrivel," said Mrs. Borkowski. "Phhhhtttt."

Which was maybe—Raymie wasn't sure—the sound a soul made when it shriveled.

But as Raymie stood in Ida Nee's backyard, next to Louisiana and Beverly, it did not feel like her soul was shriveling at all.

It felt like it was filling up—becoming larger, brighter, more certain.

Down at the lake, on the edge of the dock, Ida Nee was twirling her baton. It flashed and glimmered. She threw it very high in the air.

The baton looked like a needle.

It looked like a secret, narrow and bright and alone, glittering in the blue sky.

Raymie remembered the words from earlier: *I'm sorry I betrayed you.*

She turned to Louisiana and asked, "Who is Archie?"

Six

"Well, I'll just begin at the beginning since that's always the best place to begin," said Louisiana.

Beverly snorted.

"Once upon a time," said Louisiana, "in a land very far away and also surprisingly close by, there lived a cat named Archie Elefante, who was much admired and loved and who was also known as King of the Cats. But then darkness fell—"

"Why don't you just say what happened," said Beverly.

"All right, if you want me to, I will just say it. We betrayed him."

"How?" asked Raymie.

"We had to take Archie to the Very Friendly Animal Center because we couldn't afford to feed him anymore," said Louisiana.

"What Very Friendly Animal Center?" asked Beverly. "I've never heard of any Very Friendly Animal Center."

"I can't believe you've never heard of the Very Friendly Animal Center. It's a place where they will feed Archie three times a day and scratch him behind the ears exactly the way he likes. Still, I never should have left him there. It was a betrayal. I betrayed him."

Raymie's heart thudded. *Betrayed.*

"But don't worry," said Louisiana. She put her hand on her chest and took a deep breath. She smiled a dazzling smile. "I've entered the Little Miss Central Florida Tire 1975 contest, and I'm going to win that one thousand nine hundred and seventy-five dollars and save myself from the county home and get Archie back from the Very Friendly Animal Center and never be terrified again."

Raymie's soul stopped being a tent.

"You're going to compete in the Little Miss Central Florida Tire contest?" she asked.

"Yes, I am," said Louisiana. "And I feel like my chances at winning are very good because I come from a show-business background."

Raymie's soul became smaller, tighter. It turned into something hard, like a pebble.

"As I said before, my parents were the Flying Elefantes." Louisiana bent and picked up her baton. "They were famous."

Beverly rolled her eyes at Raymie.

"It's true. My parents traveled all over the world," said Louisiana. "They had suitcases with their names printed on them. *The Flying Elefantes.* That's what their suitcases said." Louisiana stretched out her baton and moved it around as if she were writing golden words in the air above their heads. "Their name was written on every suitcase in script, and the F and the Y had very long tails. I like long tails."

"I'm in that contest, too," said Raymie.

"What contest?" asked Louisiana. She blinked.

"The Little Miss Central Florida Tire contest," said Raymie.

"My goodness," said Louisiana. She blinked again.

"I'm going to sabotage that contest," said Beverly. She looked at Raymie and then she looked at Louisiana, and then she reached into her shorts and took out a pocketknife. She unfolded the blade. It looked like a very sharp knife.

Suddenly, even though the sun was shining high in the sky, the world seemed less bright.

Old Mrs. Borkowski said all the time that the sun could not be relied on.

"What is the sun?" said Mrs. Borkowski. "I will tell you. The sun is nothing but a dying star. Someday, it will go out. Phhhhtttt."

Phhhhtttt was actually something that Mrs. Borkowski said often and about a lot of things.

"What are you going to do with that knife?" asked Louisiana.

"I told you," said Beverly. "I am going to sabotage the contest. I am going to sabotage everything." She slashed the knife through the air.

"Oh, my goodness," said Louisiana.

"That's right," said Beverly. She smiled a very small smile, and then she folded up the knife and put it back in the pocket of her shorts.

Seven

They walked together up to Ida Nee's circular driveway.

Ida Nee was still down on the dock, marching back and forth and twirling her baton and talking to herself. Raymie could hear her voice — a low, angry murmur — but she could not understand what she was saying.

"I hate Little Miss contests," said Beverly. "I hate bows and ribbons and batons and all of it. I hate spangly things. My mother has entered me into every Little Miss contest there ever was, and

I'm tired of it. And that is why I'm going to sabotage this one."

"But there's one thousand nine hundred and seventy-five dollars to win," said Louisiana. "That is a king's ransom. That's an untold fortune! Do you know how much tuna fish you can buy for one thousand nine hundred and seventy-five dollars?"

"No," said Beverly. "And I don't care."

"Tuna fish is very high in protein," said Louisiana. "In the county home, they only serve you bologna sandwiches. Bologna is not good for people with swampy lungs."

This conversation was interrupted by a loud noise. A station wagon with wood paneling on its side was coming toward Ida Nee's circular driveway very fast. The driver's-side back door of the station wagon was partially unhinged; it was swinging open and then slamming shut again.

"Here is Granny," said Louisiana.

"Where?" said Raymie.

Because it truly did not appear that anybody

was driving the car. It was like the headless horse-man, only with a station wagon instead of a horse.

And then Raymie saw two hands on the steer-ing wheel, and just as the station wagon pulled into the driveway, spraying gravel and dust, a voice called out, "Louisiana Elefante, get into the car!"

"I have to go now," said Louisiana.

"It sure seems that way," said Beverly.

"It was nice to meet you," said Raymie.

"Hurry!" shouted the voice from inside the station wagon. "Marsha Jean is somewhere close behind. I'm certain of it. I can feel her malevolent presence."

"Oh, my goodness," said Louisiana. She got in the backseat and tried to pull the broken door closed. "If Marsha Jean shows up," she shouted at Raymie and Beverly, "tell her you haven't seen me. Don't allow her to write anything down on her clipboard. And tell her that you don't know my whereabouts."

"We don't know your whereabouts," said Beverly.

"Who is Marsha Jean?" asked Raymie.

"Quit asking her questions," said Beverly. "It just gives her an excuse to make up a story."

The station wagon shot forward. The back door swung open, then shut with a loud bang and stayed closed. The car accelerated at an alarming rate, the engine roaring and groaning, and then the station wagon disappeared entirely, and Raymie and Beverly were left standing together in a cloud that was composed of dust and gravel and exhaust.

Phhhhtttt, as Mrs. Borkowski would say.

Phhhhtttt.

Eight

"They seem like criminals to me," said Beverly. "That girl and her almost-invisible granny. They remind me of Bonnie and Clyde."

Raymie nodded, even though Louisiana and her grandmother did not remind her of anyone else she had ever seen or heard of.

"Do you even know who Bonnie and Clyde were?" asked Beverly.

"Bank robbers?" said Raymie.

"That's right," said Beverly. "Criminals. Those two look like they could rob a bank. And what kind of name is Louisiana, anyway? Louisiana is the name of a state. It's not what you call a person. That girl is probably operating under an assumed name. She's probably running from the law. That's why she seems so afraid in that rabbity kind of way. I tell you what: Fear is a big waste of time. I'm not afraid of anything."

Beverly threw her baton up high in the air and caught it with a professional snap of her wrist.

Raymie felt her heart clench in disbelief.

"You already know how to twirl a baton," she said.

"So what?" said Beverly.

"Why are you even taking lessons?"

"I guess that is exactly none of your business. Why are you taking lessons?"

"Because I need to win the contest."

"I told you," said Beverly, "there's not going to be a contest. Not if I can help it. I've got all kinds of sabotaging skills. Right now, I'm reading a book on safecracking that was written by a criminal named J. Frederick Murphy. Ever heard of him?"

Raymie shook her head.

"Didn't think so," said Beverly. "My dad gave me the book. He knows all the criminal ways. I'm teaching myself how to crack a safe."

"Isn't your father a cop?" asked Raymie.

"Yeah," said Beverly. "He is. What's your point? I can already pick a lock. Have you ever picked a lock?"

"No," said Raymie.

"Didn't think so," said Beverly again.

She threw the baton up in the air and caught it in her grubby hand. She made twirling a baton look easy and impossible at the same time.

It was terrible to behold.

Suddenly, everything seemed pointless.

Raymie's plan to bring her father home wasn't much of a plan at all. What was she doing? She didn't know. She was alone, lost, cast adrift.

I'm sorry I betrayed you.

Phhhhtttt.

Sabotage.

"Aren't you afraid that you'll get caught?" said Raymie to Beverly.

"I told you already," said Beverly. "I'm not afraid of anything."

"Nothing?" asked Raymie.

"Nothing," said Beverly. She stared at Raymie so hard that her face changed. Her eyes glowed.

"Tell me a secret," whispered Beverly.

"What?" said Raymie.

Beverly looked away from Raymie. She shrugged. She threw the baton up and caught it and then threw it back in the air again. And while the baton was suspended between the sky and the gravel, Beverly said, "I told you to tell me a secret."

Beverly caught the baton. She looked at Raymie.

And who knows why?

Raymie told her.

She said, "My father ran away with a dental hygienist. He left in the middle of the night."

This was not necessarily a secret, but the words were terrible and true and it hurt to say them.

"People are doing that pathetic kind of thing all the time," said Beverly. "Creeping down hallways in the dark with their shoes in their hand, leaving without telling anyone good-bye."

Raymie didn't know if her father had crept down the hallway with his shoes in his hand, but he had certainly left without telling her good-bye. Considering this fact, she felt a pang of something. What was it? Outrage? Disbelief? Sorrow?

"It makes me really, really mad," said Beverly.

She took her baton and started beating the rubber tip of it into the gravel of the driveway. Small rocks leaped up in the air, desperate to escape Beverly's wrath.

Wham, wham, wham.

Beverly beat the gravel, and Raymie looked on in admiration and fear. She had never seen anyone so angry.

There was a lot of dust.

A car painted a brilliant, glittering blue

appeared on the horizon and pulled into the driveway and coasted to a stop.

Beverly ignored the car.

She kept beating the gravel.

It didn't look like she intended to stop until
she had reduced the whole world to dust.

Nine

"Stop that!" shouted the woman behind the wheel of the car.

Beverly did not stop. She kept whamming away.

"I paid good money for that baton," the woman said to Raymie. "Make her stop."

"Me?" said Raymie.

"Yes, you," said the woman. "Who else is standing here besides you? Get that baton away from her."

The woman had green eye shadow on her eyelids and big, fake eyelashes and also a lot of rouge on her cheeks. But underneath the rouge and the eye shadow and the fake eyelashes, she looked very familiar. She looked like Beverly Tapinski, except older. And angrier. If that was possible.

"Why do I have to do everything?" said the woman.

This was the kind of question that had no answer, the kind of question that adults seemed to be overly fond of asking.

Before Raymie could even attempt some sort of response, the woman was out of the car and had hold of Beverly's baton and was pulling on it and Beverly was pulling back.

More dust rose up in the air.

"Let go," said Beverly.

"You let go," said the woman, who was surely Beverly's mother, even though she wasn't really acting like a mother.

"Stop this nonsense immediately!"

This command issued from Ida Nee, who had

appeared out of nowhere and who was standing in front of them with her white boots glowing and her baton stretched out in front of her like a sword. She looked like an avenging angel in a Sunday-school storybook.

Beverly and the woman stopped wrestling.

"What is going on here, Rhonda?" said Ida Nee.

"Nothing," said the woman.

"Can't you control your daughter?" said Ida Nee.

"She started it," said Beverly.

"Get out of here, both of you," said Ida Nee. She pointed her baton at the car. "And don't come back until you can behave properly. You should be ashamed of yourself, Rhonda, a champion twirler like you."

Beverly got in the back of the car, and her mother got in the front. They both slammed their doors at the same time.

"See you tomorrow," said Raymie as the car pulled out of the driveway.

"Ha!" said Beverly. "You're never going to see me again."

For some reason, these words felt like a punch to the stomach. They felt like someone sneaking down a hallway in the middle of the night, carrying their shoes in their hand — leaving without saying good-bye.

Raymie turned away from the car and looked at Ida Nee, who shook her head, marched past Raymie, and went into her baton-twirling office (which was really just a garage) and closed the door.

Raymie's soul was not a tent. It was not even a pebble.

Her soul, it seemed, had disappeared entirely.

After a long time, or what seemed like a long time, Raymie's mother arrived.

"How were the lessons?" she asked when Raymie got in the car.

"Complicated," said Raymie.

"Everything is complicated," said her mother.

"I can't even begin to imagine why you would want to learn how to twirl a baton. Last summer, it was the lifesaving lessons. This summer, it's twirling. None of it makes any sense to me."

Raymie looked down at the baton in her lap. I *have a plan*, she wanted to say. *And the baton twirling is part of the plan.* She closed her eyes and imagined her father in a booth, in a diner, sitting across from Lee Ann Dickerson.

She imagined her father opening the paper and discovering that she was Little Miss Central Florida Tire. Wouldn't he be impressed? Wouldn't he want to come home immediately? And wouldn't Lee Ann Dickerson be amazed and jealous?

"What could your father possibly see in that woman?" said Raymie's mother, almost as if she knew what Raymie was thinking. "What could he see in her?"

Raymie added this question to the list of impossible, unanswerable questions that adults seemed inclined to ask her.

She thought about Mr. Staphopoulos, her

lifesaving coach from the summer before. He was not the kind of man who asked questions that didn't have answers.

Mr. Staphopoulos only ever asked one question: "Are you going to be a problem causer or a problem solver?"

And the answer was obvious.

You had to be a problem solver.

Ten

Mr. Staphopoulos had fur on his toes and fur all down his back. He wore a silver whistle around his neck. Raymie didn't think that he ever took the whistle off.

Mr. Staphopoulos was very passionate about people not drowning.

"Land is an afterthought, people!" That was what Mr. Staphopoulos said to all his Lifesaving 101 students. "The world is made of water, and drowning is an ever-present danger. We must help each other. Let's be problem solvers together."

Then Mr. Staphopoulos would blow his whistle, throw Edgar in the water, and the life-saving lesson would begin.

Edgar was the drowning dummy. He was five feet three inches tall. He was dressed in jeans and a checked button-down shirt. He had buttons for eyes, and his smile was drawn on with a red permanent marker. He was stuffed with cotton that never dried out properly, and there were stones sewn into his hands and feet and stomach so that he would sink. He smelled of mildew — a sweet, sad kind of smell.

Mr. Staphopoulos had made Edgar. He had designed him to drown.

It seemed like a strange reason to be called into the world — to drown, to be saved, to drown again.

It also seemed strange to Raymie that Edgar was doomed to smile through the whole thing.

If she had made Edgar, she would have put a more quizzical look on his face.

But in any case, Edgar and Mr. Staphopoulos

were both gone now. They had moved to North Carolina at the end of last summer.

Raymie had seen them in the parking lot of the Tag and Bag Grocery the day they left. All of Mr. Staphopoulos's belongings were packed into his station wagon, and some things were even tied on top. Edgar was sitting in the backseat, staring straight ahead. He was smiling, of course. Mr. Staphopoulos was just getting into the car.

Raymie called out, "Good-bye, Mr. Staphopoulos."

"Raymie," he said, turning around. "Raymie Clarke." He closed the door of the station wagon and walked toward her. He put his hand on her head.

It was hot in the Tag and Bag parking lot. There were seagulls whirling and screeching, and Mr. Staphopoulos's hand on top of her head was heavy and light at the same time.

Mr. Staphopoulos was wearing khaki pants and flip-flops. Raymie could see the fur on his feet. The whistle was around his neck, and the sun reflected

Eleven

At home, after the very strange baton-twirling class, Raymie sat in her room with the door closed and worked on the Little Miss Central Florida Tire application. It was a two-page, mimeographed form, and it was obvious that Mr. Pitt, the owner of Central Florida Tire, had typed the form himself. He was not a very good typist. The application was full of errors, which for some reason made the whole enterprise (the contest and the hope that Raymie would win it and the further hope that winning it would bring her father home) seem dubious.

off of it and made the whistle into a little circle of light. It looked like something in the center of Mr. Staphopoulos was on fire.

The sun glinted off the abandoned grocery carts and made them magical, beautiful. Everything shimmered. The seagulls called out. Raymie thought that something wonderful was going to happen.

But nothing happened except that Mr. Staphopoulos kept his hand on her head for what seemed like a long time, and then he lifted his hand and squeezed her shoulder and said, "Good-bye, Raymie."

Just that.

"Good-bye, Raymie."

Why did those words matter so much?

Raymie didn't know.

The first question was in all-capital letters. It said: DO YOU WANT TO BECOME LITTLE MISS CENTRAL FLORIDA TIRE 1975?

There was no space for an answer to this question; still, it was a question and Raymie felt like it would be best to answer it, since the application said, "Make sure yu answer ALL Questions."

Raymie squeezed in the word YES right after the question mark. She used all-capital letters. She thought about adding an exclamation mark, but decided against it.

And then she filled in her name: Raymie Clarke.

And her address: 1213 Borton Street, Lister, Fla.

And then her age: 10.

She wondered if Louisiana and Beverly were sitting in their rooms filling out their applications. Did you have to fill out an application for a contest if you intended to sabotage the contest?

Raymie closed her eyes and saw Louisiana writing the words "The Flying Elefantes" in the air with her baton. How could Raymie compete against somebody from a show-business back-ground?

Raymie opened her eyes and looked out the window. Old Mrs. Borkowski was sitting in a lawn chair in the middle of the road. Her shoes were untied. Her face was lifted up to the sun.

Raymie's mother said that Mrs. Borkowski was as crazy as a loon.

Raymie didn't know if this was true or not. But it seemed to her that Mrs. Borkowski knew things, important things. Some of the things she knew, she told. And some of the things she knew, she refused to tell, saying nothing but "Phhhhtttt" when Raymie asked for more information.

Old Mrs. Borkowski probably knew who the Flying Elefantes were.

Raymie looked back down at the application. It said, "Please list all of your GOOD DEEdS. Use a separate sheet of paper if necessary."

Good deeds? What good deeds?

Raymie's stomach clenched. She got up from the desk and left her room and went out the front door and walked into the middle of the street. She stood in front of Mrs. Borkowski's lawn chair.

"What?" said Mrs. Borkowski without opening her eyes.

"I'm filling out an application," said Raymie.

"Yes, and so?"

"I'm supposed to do good deeds," said Raymie.

"One time," said Mrs. Borkowski. She smacked her lips. Her eyes were still closed. "One time a something happened."

Obviously, Mrs. Borkowski intended to tell a story. Raymie sat down in the middle of the road at Mrs. Borkowski's feet. The pavement was warm. She looked at Mrs. Borkowski's untied shoes.

Mrs. Borkowski never tied her shoes.

She was too old to reach her feet.

"One time a something happened," said Mrs. Borkowski again. "I was on a boat at sea, and I saw a baby get snatched from his mother's arms. By a bird. A gigantic seabird."

"Is this a story about a good deed?" asked Raymie.

"It was terrible, how the mother screamed."

"But the mother got the baby back, right?"

"From a gigantic seabird? Never," said Mrs. Borkowski. "Those gigantic seabirds, they keep what they take. Also, they steal buttons. And hairpins." Mrs. Borkowski lowered her head and opened her eyes and looked at Raymie. She blinked. Mrs. Borkowski had very sad, extremely watery eyes. "The wings of the seabird were huge. They looked like they belonged to an angel."

"So was the seabird actually an angel? Was it doing a good deed and saving the baby?"

"Phhhhtttt," said Mrs. Borkowski. She waved her hand through the air. "Who knows? I'm only telling you what happened. What I saw. Make of it what you will. Tomorrow, you come over and cut my toenails, and I will give you some of that divinity candy, okay?"

"Okay," said Raymie.

Did cutting Mrs. Borkowski's toenails count as a good deed? Probably not. Mrs. Borkowski always gave Raymie candy in exchange for the toenail cutting, and if you got paid for something, it couldn't be a good deed.

Mrs. Borkowski closed her eyes. She tilted her head back again. After a while, she started to snore.

Raymie got up and went in the house and into the kitchen.

She picked up the phone and dialed her father's office.

"Clarke Family Insurance," said Mrs. Sylvester in her cartoon-bird voice. "How may we protect you?"

Raymie said nothing.

Mrs. Sylvester cleared her throat. "Clarke Family Insurance," she said again. "How may we protect you?"

It was nice to hear Mrs. Sylvester ask, "How may we protect you?" a second time. Actually, Raymie thought that she would like to hear Mrs. Sylvester ask the question several hundred times a day. It was such a friendly question. It was a question that promised good things.

"Mrs. Sylvester?" she said.

"Yes, dear," said Mrs. Sylvester.

Raymie closed her eyes and imagined the gigantic jar of candy corn sitting on Mrs. Sylvester's desk. Sometimes, in the late afternoon, the sun shone directly on the jar and lit it up so that it looked like a lamp.

Raymie wondered if that was happening now.

Behind Mrs. Sylvester's desk was the door to Raymie's father's office. That door would be closed, and the office would be empty. No one would be sitting at her father's desk, because her father was gone.

Raymie tried to conjure up his face. She tried to imagine him sitting in his office at his desk.

She couldn't do it.

She felt a wave of panic. Her father had only been gone for two days, and she couldn't remember his face. She had to bring him back!

She remembered why she was calling.

"Mrs. Sylvester," she said, "you have to perform good deeds for the contest."

"Oh, honey," said Mrs. Sylvester, "that is no problem at all. You just go down the street to the

Golden Glen and offer to read to one of the residents. The elderly love to be read to."

Did the elderly love to be read to? Raymie wasn't sure. Old Mrs. Borkowski was elderly and what she always wanted Raymie to do was to clip her toenails.

"How was your first baton-twirling lesson?" asked Mrs. Sylvester.

"It was interesting," said Raymie.

An image of Louisiana Elefante falling to her knees flashed through her head. This image was followed by one of Beverly Tapinski and her mother fighting over the baton in a cloud of gravel dust.

"Isn't it exciting to be learning something new?" said Mrs. Sylvester.

"Yes," said Raymie.

"How's your mother doing, dear?" said Mrs. Sylvester.

"She's sitting on the couch in the sunroom right now. She does that a lot. Mostly, that's what she does. She doesn't really do anything else. She just sits there."

"Well," said Mrs. Sylvester. There was a long pause. "It will be fine. You'll see. We all do what we can do."

"Okay," said Raymie.

Louisiana's words floated through her head. *I'm too terrified to go on.*

Raymie didn't say the words out loud, but she felt them pass through her. And Mrs. Sylvester — kind, bird-voiced Mrs. Sylvester — must have felt them, too, because she said, "You just select a suitable book for sharing, dear, and then go down to the Golden Glen. They will be very glad to see you there. You just do what you can do, okay? Everything will be fine. It will all work out right in the end."

Twelve

It wasn't until Raymie hung up the phone that she wondered what Mrs. Sylvester meant by a "suitable" book.

She walked into the living room and stood on the yellow shag carpet and stared at the bookcase. All the books were brown and serious. They were her father's books. What if he came back home and one was missing? She felt like maybe it would be best to leave them alone.

Raymie went into her room. The shelves over her bed held rocks and seashells and stuffed animals and books. *The Borrowers?* No, it was too unlikely. No normal adult would believe in tiny people who lived under the floorboards. *Paddington Bear?* Something about the book seemed too bright and silly for the seriousness of a nursing home. *Little House in the Big Woods?* A really old person had probably lived through all that history and wouldn't want to hear about it again.

And then Raymie saw *A Bright and Shining Path: The Life of Florence Nightingale.* This was a book that Edward Option had given her on the last day of school. Mr. Option was the school librarian. He was very skinny and extremely tall. He had to duck his head to enter and exit the George Mason Willamette Elementary School library.

Mr. Option looked too young and uncertain to be a librarian.

Also, his ties were too wide, and they were all painted with strange and lonely pictures of deserted beaches, haunted-looking forests, or UFOs.

Sometimes, when he held up a book, Mr. Option's hands shook with nervousness. Or maybe it was excitement.

In any case, on the last day of school, Edward Option had said to Raymie, "You are such a good reader, Raymie Clarke, that I wonder if you might be interested in diversifying. I have here a nonfiction book that you might enjoy."

"Okay," said Raymie, even though she had absolutely no interest in nonfiction. She liked stories.

Mr. Option held up *A Bright and Shining Path: The Life of Florence Nightingale*. On the cover, there were dozens of soldiers stretched out on their backs on what looked like a battlefield and a lady was walking in between the soldiers and carrying a lamp over her head, and the men were holding their hands out to her, begging her for something.

There was no bright and shining path anywhere in sight.

It looked like a horrible, depressing book.

"Maybe," said Mr. Option, "you could read this over the summer, and then we could talk about it together when school begins."

"Okay," said Raymie again. But she only agreed because she liked Mr. Option so much, and because he was so tall and lonely and hopeful.

She had taken the Florence Nightingale book from him and brought it home and put it on her shelf. A few days later, her father had run away with Lee Ann Dickerson and Raymie forgot all about Edward Option and his strange ties and his nonfiction book.

But maybe somebody at the Golden Glen Nursing Home would want to hear about the life of Florence Nightingale and her shining path. Maybe it was exactly what Mrs. Sylvester meant by a "suitable" book.

Maybe everything would work out right in the end.

Thirteen

The Golden Glen Nursing Home was four blocks from Raymie's house. Raymie could have ridden her bike, but she decided to walk so that she would have time to flex her toes and isolate her objectives.

Every day in Lifesaving 101, Mr. Staphopoulos had all the students stand on the dock and flex their toes and isolate their objectives. Mr. Staphopoulos believed that flexing your toes cleared your mind and that once your mind was clear, it was easy to isolate your objectives and figure out what to do next. For instance: save whoever was drowning.

"What is my objective?" whispered Raymie. She stopped. She flexed her toes inside her tennis shoes. "My objective is to do a good deed. And also to become Little Miss Central Florida Tire so that my father will come back home."

Her stomach clenched up. What if Louisiana won? What if Beverly sabotaged the contest? What if Raymie's father never came home, no matter what Raymie did? A gigantic seabird flew through Raymie's brain, its talons extended.

"No, no, no," she whispered. She flexed her toes. She cleared her mind. She isolated her objectives. *Do a good deed,* she thought. *Become Little Miss Central Florida Tire. Do a good deed. Do a good deed.*

After a lot of toe flexing, Raymie arrived at the Golden Glen and discovered that the door was locked.

There was a sign that read THIS DOOR IS LOCKED.

PLEASE RING THE BELL FOR ADMITTANCE. An arrow on the sign pointed to a button.

Raymie pressed the button and heard a bell ringing somewhere deep inside the building. She waited. She flexed her toes.

An intercom crackled to life. "This is Martha speaking. It's a golden day at the Golden Glen. How may I assist you?"

"Hello," said Raymie.

"Hello," said the woman named Martha.

"Um," said Raymie. "I'm here to do a good deed."

"Isn't that wonderful?" said Martha.

Raymie wasn't sure if this was a statement or a question, so she said nothing in response. There was a long silence. Raymie said, "I brought a book about Florence Nightingale."

"The nurse?" said Martha.

"Um," said Raymie. "She has a lamp. And the book is called *A Bright and Shining Path: The Life of Florence Nightingale.*"

"Fascinating," said Martha.

The intercom gave a lonely crackle.

Raymie took a deep breath. She said, "Can I come inside and read the book to someone?"

"Of course," said Martha. "I'll buzz you in."

There was a long, loud buzz, and Raymie heard the door unlatch. She reached forward and grabbed the handle and entered the Golden Glen. Inside, it smelled like floor wax and old fruit salad and something else, a smell that Raymie did not want to think about too much.

A woman with a blue sweater draped over her shoulders stood behind a counter at the end of the hallway. She smiled at Raymie. "Hello," she said. "I'm Martha."

"I am the person who was going to read to someone?" said Raymie. She held up Florence Nightingale.

"Of course, of course," said Martha. She stepped out from behind the counter. "Come with me."

She took Raymie's hand and led her up a flight

of stairs and into a room where the floor was polished and shining so brightly that it didn't look
like a floor at all. It looked like a lake.

Raymie's heart thudded and skipped.

She had the feeling that she was going to
understand things, finally, at last. She had this feeling often, that some truth was going to be revealed
to her. She had felt it in the Tag and Bag parking
lot with Mr. Staphopoulos when he was telling her
good-bye. She had felt it earlier that day, standing
with Beverly and Louisiana in Ida Nee's backyard.
Sometimes she felt it when she was sitting at Mrs.
Borkowski's feet.

But so far, the feeling had never really panned
out.

The truth had never revealed itself.

But maybe this time would be different.

The room expanded. The brightness got
brighter. Raymie thought about safecracking and
sabotaging and the Flying Elefantes. She thought
about her father sitting in the diner with Lee Ann
Dickerson. She thought about Edgar the drowning

dummy and gigantic seabirds with wings like angels. She thought about all the things she didn't understand but wanted to.

And then the sun went behind a cloud and the lake turned back into a floor and Martha said, "Let's just go talk to Isabelle," and it was all over. The feeling of almost understanding was gone, and Raymie didn't know any more than she had before.

Martha led Raymie over to an old lady sitting in a wheelchair parked by a window.

"Isabelle's eyesight is not what it once was," said Martha, "so she is not able to read like she used to."

"I can read just fine," said Isabelle.

"Well, that is just not true, Isabelle," said Martha. "You are as blind as a bat."

Isabelle made a fist with her right hand and brought it down on the arm of the wheelchair. *Wham, wham, wham.* "Don't bother me, Martha," she said. She was a tiny woman and her hair was pure white, and someone had braided it into a complicated crown on top of her head so that she looked like a fairy godmother. Her eyes were very blue.

Martha turned to Raymie. "What's your name, child?" she asked.

Raymie had never been called "child" before. She knew that she was a child, of course, but there was something oddly comforting about someone addressing the situation directly.

"I'm Raymie," she said.

"Isabelle," said Martha. "This is Raymie."

"So what?" said Isabelle.

"She would like to read to you about the life of Florence Nightingale."

"You're kidding," said Isabelle.

"Isabelle," said Martha, "please. The child wants to do a good deed."

Isabelle looked up at Raymie. Her eyes were bright. She didn't look like she was as blind as a bat. It was more like she had X-ray vision.

Raymie could feel Isabelle looking right inside her.

She squinched up her soul as small as she could and pushed it to one side, so that it was hidden.

"A good deed?" said Isabelle. "Why do you want to do a good deed? What is your purpose exactly?"

Her purpose? Was that the same thing as an objective?

Raymie flexed her toes.

"Just, um, to do a good deed," she said.

Isabelle kept staring at her. Raymie stared back. She made her soul smaller and smaller. She imagined it becoming as tiny as the period at the end of a sentence. No one would ever find it.

"Fine," said Isabelle after what seemed like a very long time. "Who cares? Read to me about Florence Nightingale."

"Isn't that wonderful?" said Martha to Raymie. "Isabelle would like to learn about Florence Nightingale."

Fourteen

"I couldn't care less about Florence Nightingale," said Isabelle as Raymie pushed her wheelchair down a long hallway lined with closed doors. "Do-gooders don't interest me. They are the least interesting people on the planet. And Florence Nightingale was a do-gooder if there ever was one."

"Okay," said Raymie, because she couldn't think of anything else to say. Also, it was hard to talk. She was out of breath from pushing the wheelchair. Isabelle was heavier than she looked.

"Faster," said Isabelle.

"What?" said Raymie.

"Go faster," said Isabelle.

Raymie tried to push the wheelchair faster. She could feel little pinpricks of sweat on her upper lip. Her arms hurt. So did her legs.

"Take my hand!" shouted a terrible voice from behind one of the closed doors.

"What was that?" said Raymie. She stopped pushing the wheelchair.

"What are you doing?" said Isabelle. "Why are you stopping?"

"Take my hand!" screamed the voice again. Raymie's heart jumped up high in her chest, and then sank down low.

"Who is that?" asked Raymie.

"That's Alice Nebbley," said Isabelle. "Ignore her. She knows one sentence, and she says it day and night. The monotony of her request is too horrible to bear."

To Raymie, the voice didn't sound like it belonged to someone named Alice. Instead, it sounded like the voice of a troll who was standing under a bridge hoping that an unsuspecting billy goat would walk by.

Raymie's heart was pounding somewhere deep inside of her now. It felt as if it had moved position permanently — from her chest to her stomach. She thought how nice it would be if she were like Beverly Tapinski and afraid of nothing.

Raymie took a deep breath and started to push the wheelchair again.

"That's right," said Isabelle. "The trick is to keep moving. Never stop moving."

Fifteen

Isabelle's room had a single bed in it and a rocking chair and a nightstand with a clock on it. There was an afghan on the rocking chair. The walls were painted white. The clock was ticking very loudly.

"Should I sit down?" asked Raymie.

"What do I care?" said Isabelle.

Raymie sat in the rocking chair, but she held herself very still. It didn't seem like a good time to rock. "Should I read to you now?" she asked. She held up Florence Nightingale.

"Do not," said Isabelle, "read to me from that book."

"Okay," said Raymie. She flexed her toes. She tried to isolate her objectives, but for the life of her, she couldn't think of what to do next. Should she just leave?

"Take my hand!" shouted Alice Nebbley.

The voice was not as loud as it had been in the hallway, but it was still loud enough to make Raymie jump.

"This place," said Isabelle.

And then, from far away, there came the sound of music. It was beautiful, sad music. Someone was playing the piano. For some reason, the song made Raymie think of the Flying Elefantes (whoever they were) and their luggage.

"I can't stand it," said Isabelle. She put her head in her hands.

"Should I go?" asked Raymie.

Isabelle raised her head and narrowed her eyes. "Can you write?"

"Write?" said Raymie.

"Letters," said Isabelle. "Words. On a piece of paper." She balled up her fist and pounded it on the arm of the wheelchair. "Can you put words on paper? Oh, the frustration of this world!"

"Yes," said Raymie.

"Good," said Isabelle. "Get the notepad from the top drawer of the nightstand. And the pen. You write what I say, exactly what I say."

Was writing for someone a good deed? It had to be. Raymie got up and retrieved the pen and the notepad. She sat back down.

"To the management," said Isabelle.

Raymie looked at her.

"Write it," said Isabelle, pounding her fist on the wheelchair arm again. "Write it, write it."

"Take my hand!" shouted Alice Nebbley.

Raymie bent her head. She wrote, *To the management*. Her hand was shaking.

"There is entirely too much Chopin played in this establishment," said Isabelle.

Raymie looked up.

"Write that, too," said Isabelle.

A long silence prevailed in the room.

"I don't know how to spell *Chopin*," said Raymie finally.

"What do they teach you in those schools?" asked Isabelle.

This, Raymie knew, was another impossible, unanswerable adult question. She waited.

"He was a musician," said Isabelle. "An entirely too gloomy one. *Chopin* is a proper name. Therefore, it begins with a capital C and is followed by a lowercase h."

And so they continued; by the end, Raymie had written a letter of complaint for Isabelle, detailing how the Golden Glen janitor played the wrong kind of music on the common-room piano. According to Isabelle, the music of Chopin was too mournful, and the janitor needed to stop playing it because the world was mournful enough on its own. The Golden Glen, in particular, was too mournful to be borne, according to Isabelle.

It was a very long letter.

And when Raymie was done writing it,

Isabelle made Raymie push her wheelchair out of the room and down the hallway and back to the common room, where the floor was just a floor and not a glowing lake, and where there was a wooden box with the word SUGGESTIONS printed on its side in silver stick-on letters.

"Drop it in," said Isabelle.

"Me?" said Raymie.

"You wrote it, didn't you?" said Isabelle.

Raymie put the letter in the box.

"There," said Isabelle. "You wanted to do a good deed. You did a good deed."

Writing a letter of complaint about mournful music didn't seem like a good deed at all. It seemed like the opposite of a good deed.

"Take me back to my room," said Isabelle. "I've had enough."

Raymie thought that she had had enough, too. She turned the wheelchair around and headed back to Isabelle's room.

"Take my hand!" shouted Alice Nebbley as they made their way down the hallway.

"Close the door when you leave," said Isabelle after Raymie had wheeled her into her room. "And do not return. I am not interested in people doing good deeds. Good deeds are pointless, in any case. Nothing changes. Nothing matters."

The sun was trying to make its way through the one small window in Isabelle's room. Raymie stood in the doorway holding Florence close to her chest, as if the book could protect her. Which it couldn't, of course. She knew that.

Everything seemed bleak, impossible.

"Archie, I'm sorry I betrayed you," said Raymie without really meaning to say it.

"Yes, well, poor Archie, alas Archie. And alas your betrayal of him," said Isabelle, "whoever he is."

"He's a cat," said Raymie.

Isabelle stared at Raymie with her bright-blue eyes. "Is that why you want to do a good deed, because you betrayed a cat?"

"No," said Raymie. "My father left."

"And?"

"I'm working to get him back," said Raymie.

"With good deeds?" said Isabelle.

"Yes," said Raymie. Maybe it was because of Isabelle's X-ray vision, or maybe it was because of her lack of sympathy; for some reason, Raymie told Isabelle the truth. "I'm going to win a contest and then I will be famous, and he will see my picture in the paper and he will have to come home."

"I see," said Isabelle.

Just then, the sun managed to come around the corner of Isabelle's window and throw itself into a small square of light on the floor. It was very bright. It shimmered. It looked like the window to another universe.

"Look," said Raymie. She pointed at the sun patch.

"I see," said Isabelle. "I see."

Sixteen

"Take my hand!" shouted Alice Nebbley as Raymie walked down the hallway.

Raymie stopped. She listened. She flexed her toes. And then she started walking again. She followed the sound of Alice's voice.

Raymie needed to do a good deed, plus she needed to make up for the bad deed she had just done. That meant she had to do the bravest, best deed she could think of, the deed she least wanted to do.

She had to go into Alice Nebbley's room and ask her if she wanted to be read to.

It was a terrifying prospect.

Raymie looked down at her feet. She made herself put one foot in front of the other. She concentrated on Alice's voice.

The voice led her to a door with the number 323 on it, and underneath the number was a white card. *Alice Nebbley* was written on the card in black ink. The letters of the name were shaky and uncertain, like maybe Alice Nebbley had written them herself.

Raymie flexed her toes. She knocked.

And when no one answered, Raymie took a deep breath, grabbed the doorknob and turned it, then stepped inside. The room was dark, but Raymie could see that someone was in the bed.

"Mrs. Nebbley?" whispered Raymie.

There was no answer.

Raymie stepped farther into the room.

"Mrs. Nebbley?" she said again, a little bit

louder this time. She could hear whoever was in bed breathing in a raspy, strangled kind of way.

"Um," said Raymie. "I'm here to do a good deed? Would you like to hear about a bright and shining path and, um, Florence Nightingale . . . Mrs. Nebbley?"

"Arrrrrggggghhhhhhh!" screamed Alice Nebbley.

It was the most terrifying noise Raymie had ever heard in her life. It was a sound of pure pain, pure need. Alice Nebbley's scream pierced something inside of Raymie. She felt her soul whoosh away into nothingness.

"I cannnnoooottttt!" shouted Alice Nebbley. "Give meeeee." A hand rose out of the covers. It was reaching for something. It was reaching for her — Raymie Clarke!

Raymie jumped, and *A Bright and Shining Path: The Life of Florence Nightingale* leaped out of her hands and flew into the air and skittered under Alice Nebbley's bed.

Raymie screamed.

Alice Nebbley screamed back. "Arrrrgggghh! I cannot, cannot, cannot bear the pain! Take my hand." Her hand was still extended, reaching out of the covers, searching. "Please, please, take my hand."

Raymie Clarke turned and ran.

Raymie stood for a long time on the sidewalk in front of the Golden Glen, flexing her toes and isolating her objectives.

She had to get the book back. That was her one true objective right now. It was a library book. Edward Option would be very disappointed in her if she didn't return it. She hadn't even read it, and that would disappoint him, too. And there would be fines, overdue fines!

What if she had to pay for the book?

But she couldn't go back into Alice Nebbley's room. She truly didn't know if she was brave enough to ever enter the Golden Glen again.

She thought about Isabelle's X-ray eyes.

She thought about Alice Nebbley's hand.

She thought about gigantic seabirds that snatched babies from their mothers' arms.

And then she heard Beverly Tapinski's voice: *Fear is a big waste of time. I'm not afraid of anything.*

Beverly. Beverly Tapinski and her pocketknife.

Beverly, who was afraid of nothing.

Raymie knew, suddenly, what her objective was.

She would find Beverly and ask her to help get Florence Nightingale back.

Seventeen

Finding Beverly Tapinski turned out to be surprisingly easy.

When Raymie got to baton-twirling lessons the next afternoon, Beverly was standing under the pine trees, chewing gum and staring straight ahead.

"I thought you weren't coming back," said Raymie.

Beverly said nothing.

"I'm glad you came back."

Beverly turned and looked at her. There was a bruise on her face, under her left eye.

"What happened to your face?" asked Raymie.

"Nothing happened to my face," said Beverly. She chewed her gum and looked right at Raymie. Beverly's eyes were blue. They weren't the same blue as Isabelle's; they were darker, deeper. But they had the same effect as Isabelle's eyes. Raymie felt as if they could see right through her, inside of her.

She stared back at Beverly and started trying to rearrange her soul, working to make it invisible.

And then Louisiana Elefante showed up.

She had on the same pink dress from the day before. But today she was wearing barrettes, six of them. The barrettes were scattered randomly throughout Louisiana's limp blond hair. All the barrettes were identical — made of pink, shiny plastic with little white bunnies painted on them. The bunnies looked like ghost bunnies.

"I'm not going to faint today," said Louisiana.

"Good news," said Beverly. "Got yourself some bunny barrettes, huh?"

"These are my good-luck bunnies. I forgot to

wear them yesterday, and look what happened. I'm never going to remove them from my head again. What's on your face?"

"Nothing's on my face," said Beverly.

At this point, Ida Nee came marching toward them, her white boots glowing and her baton flashing. She had on a spangled top that sparkled like fish scales. Her hair was very yellow. She looked like a mermaid in a bad mood.

"Here we go," said Beverly.

"Stand at attention!" shouted Ida Nee. "Stand up straight! That is the first rule of baton twirling, to stand as if you value yourself and your place in the world."

Raymie tried to stand up straight.

"Shoulders back, chin up, batons out in front of you!" said Ida Nee. "And we will begin." She raised her baton. And then she lowered it. She looked at Beverly. "Tapinski," she said, "are you chewing gum?"

"No."

Ida Nee lunged toward Beverly. Her baton

flashed brilliantly, violently, in the afternoon sun.

And then, unbelievably, the baton landed on Beverly's head.

Where it kind of bounced, because of the rubber tip.

Louisiana gasped.

"Don't lie to me," said Ida Nee. "Never lie to me. Spit it out."

"No," said Beverly.

"What?" said Ida Nee.

"No," said Beverly again.

"Oh, my goodness," said Louisiana. She put her hand on Raymie's arm. "Here I am wearing my lucky bunny barrettes, but I am still thinking that I might faint."

Raymie thought that she might faint, too, even though she had never fainted before and had no idea what almost fainting felt like. Louisiana held on to her arm and Raymie held on to . . . what? She didn't know. She held on to the fact that Louisiana was holding on to her, she supposed.

Ida Nee raised the baton to hit Beverly again.

Louisiana took her hand off of Raymie's arm and let out a strange noise—something between a scream and a squeak—and then she lunged forward and grabbed hold of Ida Nee's spangled midsection.

"Stop it!" shouted Louisiana. "You stop it!"

"What in the world?" said Ida Nee. "Unhand me." She tried to peel Louisiana off of her, but Louisiana held tight.

"Don't hit her again," said Louisiana. "Please don't."

Lake Clara glittered. The pine trees swayed. The world sighed and creaked, and Louisiana clung to Ida Nee as if she would never, ever let her go. "Don't hit her, don't hit her," Louisiana chanted.

"Don't be stupid," said Beverly.

This seemed like good advice, but Raymie wasn't sure exactly whom it was intended for.

"Please don't hurt her," said Louisiana. She was crying now.

"Get off me," said Ida Nee, pushing at Louisiana.

"Look," said Beverly. "I'm spitting out the gum."

She spit out the gum.

"See?" she said. "No one's going to hurt me. It's impossible to hurt me." She put down her baton and held up her hands. "Come here," she said. "It's fine." She pulled Louisiana off of Ida Nee. She patted Louisiana on the back. "See?" said Beverly again. "It's all fine. I'm fine."

Ida Nee blinked. She looked confused. "This is nonsense," she said. "And you know how I feel about nonsense." She took a deep breath and marched away, back toward the house.

And that was the end of the second baton-twirling lesson.

Eighteen

The three of them were down at the dock.

"So let me get this straight," said Beverly. "You want me to go into some old lady's room and take a book about Florence Nightingale out from under her bed."

"Yes," said Raymie.

"Because you're afraid to do it."

"She screams," said Raymie. "And it's a library book. I have to get it back."

"I want to come, too," said Louisiana.

"No," said Beverly and Raymie together.

"But why not?" said Louisiana. "We're the Three Rancheros! We're bound to each other through thick and thin."

"The three who?" asked Raymie.

"Rancheros," said Louisiana.

"It's Musketeers," said Beverly. "It's the Three Musketeers."

"No," said Louisiana. "That's them. We're us. And we're the Rancheros. We'll rescue each other."

"I don't need to be rescued," said Beverly.

"I want to come with you to the Sparkling Dell," said Louisiana.

"It's the Golden Glen," said Raymie.

"I want to help rescue the Florence Darksong book."

"Nightingale," said Raymie and Beverly at the same time.

"And when we're done doing that, we can go to the Very Friendly Animal Center and rescue Archie."

"Listen," said Beverly. "Let me tell you

something. There is no Very Friendly Animal Center. That cat is long gone."

"He's not long gone," said Louisiana. "I'll rescue him and that will be my good deed for the Little Miss Central Florida Tire 1975 contest, and my other good deed will be that I will help you get the book back. Also, I'll stop stealing canned goods with Granny."

"You steal canned goods?" said Raymie.

"Tuna fish, mostly," said Louisiana. "It's very high in protein."

"I told you," said Beverly to Raymie. "I looked at them and I could tell that they were criminals."

"We're not criminals," said Louisiana. "We're survivors. We're fighters."

At this point, there was a long silence. The three of them stared out at Lake Clara. The water glittered and sighed.

"There's a lady who drowned in this lake," said Raymie. "Her name was Clara Wingtip."

"So?" said Beverly.

"She haunts it," said Raymie. "In my father's

office, there's a photo of the lake from the air, and you can see Clara Wingtip's shadow under the water."

Beverly snorted. "I don't believe in fairy tales."

"You can hear her weeping sometimes," said Raymie. "That's what they say."

"Really?" said Louisiana. She rearranged her barrettes and put her hair behind one ear and leaned in toward the lake. "Oh," she said. "I hear it. I hear the weeping."

Beverly snorted.

Raymie listened.

She heard weeping, too.

Nineteen

"So, okay," said Beverly. "You get the book, and you get the cat. But what do I get?"

They were all on their backs on Ida Nee's dock, staring up at the sky.

"Well, what do you want?" asked Louisiana.

"I don't want anything," said Beverly.

"I don't believe you," said Louisiana. "Everybody wants something; everybody wishes."

"I don't wish. I sabotage."

"Oh, dear," said Louisiana.

Raymie said nothing.

She looked up at the impossibly bright sky and remembered how Mrs. Borkowski had told her once that if you were in a hole that was deep enough and if it was daylight and you looked up at the sky from the very deep hole, you could see stars even though it was the middle of the day.

Could that be true?

Raymie didn't know. Mrs. Borkowski dispensed a lot of questionable information.

"Phhhhtttt," said Raymie very quietly to herself.

And then she thought about how in fairy tales people got three wishes and none of the wishes ever turned out right. If the wishes came true, they came true in terrible ways. Wishes were dangerous things. That was the idea you got from fairy tales.

Maybe it was smart of Beverly not to wish.

From somewhere behind them, up at Ida Nee's house, there came a loud screeching noise, which was followed by a bang and then a thump.

"Granny is here," said Louisiana. She sat up.

"Louisiana!" someone called. "Louisiana Elefante!"

Raymie sat up, too. "Who were the Flying Elefantes?" she asked.

"I told you," said Louisiana. "They were my parents."

"But what does it mean? The flying part? What did they do?"

"Well, my goodness," said Louisiana. "They were trapeze artists, of course."

"Of course," said Beverly.

"They flew through the air with the greatest of ease. They were famous. They had personalized luggage."

"Louisiana Elefantteeeee."

"Granny's anxious," said Louisiana. "I have to go." She stood up and smoothed down the front of her dress. Her bunny barrettes glowed in the light of the sun. Each barrette looked purposeful, alive, as if it were busy receiving messages from very far away.

Louisiana smiled down at Raymie. It was a

beautiful smile. And for a minute, Louisiana almost looked like an angel, with her pink dress and the blue sky lit up behind her and all her barrettes glowing.

"They died," said Louisiana.

"What?" said Raymie.

"My parents. They died. They aren't the Flying Elefantes anymore. They're not anything anymore. They're at the bottom of the ocean. They were on a ship that sank. Maybe you heard about it?"

"We haven't heard about it," said Beverly, who was still on her back on the dock, staring up at the sky. "Why would we know about a ship sinking?"

"Well, anyway. It was long ago and far away. And it was a great tragedy. All the Flying Elefante luggage sank to the bottom of the ocean, and my parents drowned. And that is why I never learned how to swim."

"That makes sense," said Beverly.

"Now it's just Granny and me. And Marsha Jean, of course. She wants to capture me and put me in the county home, where they only ever serve you bologna to eat. It's all very terrifying when you think about it. So I try not to think about it."

"Louisiannnnnnaa!" shouted her grandmother.

Louisiana bent and picked up her baton. "I'll see you both tomorrow at the Golden Glen Happy Retirement Home on the corner of Borton Street and Grint Avenue at twelve noon sharp."

"Okay," said Raymie.

"It's not the Golden Glen Happy Retirement Home," said Beverly. "It's a nursing home."

"Good-bye, and long live the Rancheros!" shouted Louisiana as she walked away.

"Do you think her parents were really trapeze artists?" said Raymie to Beverly.

"I don't care if they were," said Beverly. "But they weren't."

"Oh," said Raymie.

From up at the house, there came the sound of the Elefante station wagon pulling away. It made a very loud noise, as if it were a broken rocket ship working to escape the earth's atmosphere.

"I should probably go up there," said Raymie. "My mother will be here soon."

"Where's your father?"

"What?" said Raymie.

"Your father. Did he come back home?" asked Beverly. The bruise on her face suddenly looked darker, meaner.

"No," said Raymie.

"I didn't think so," said Beverly.

Raymie felt her soul shrink. The sky didn't look as blue. She decided that she didn't believe at all what Mrs. Borkowski said about daylight stars and deep holes. Her mother was right. Mrs. Borkowski was as crazy as a loon.

Probably.

Phhhhtttt.

"Look," said Beverly. "Don't get all upset. That's just how things go. People leave and they don't come back. Somebody has to tell you the truth." She stood up and stretched, and then she bent down and picked up her baton. "But, listen, don't worry—we'll go and get your stupid library book from underneath the old lady's bed, because that's an easy thing to get back. That's no problem at all."

Beverly threw the baton up in the air once, twice, three times. Each time, she caught it without even looking.

"See you tomorrow, then," said Beverly Tapinski.

And she walked away.

Twenty

They met at the Golden Glen at noon the next day,
which was Saturday and not a baton-twirling day.

Louisiana got there first.

Raymie could see her standing on the corner from half a block away. She sparkled. She was
wearing an orange dress with silver sequins at the
hem and gold sequins sprinkled around its gauzy
sleeves. She had added more barrettes to her hair.
All the barrettes were pink and had bunnies on
them. Who knew that there were so many bunny
barrettes in the world?

"I am wearing some extra good-luck bunny barrettes today," said Louisiana.

"You look nice," said Raymie.

"Do you think that orange and pink go together, or is that only in my imagination?"

Raymie didn't get a chance to answer this question because Beverly arrived. She looked angry. The bruise on her face had gone from black to a sickly looking green.

"So?" said Beverly as she approached them.

Raymie wasn't sure what this question was in reference to, but she didn't take it as a good sign. She went and rang the bell before Beverly could change her mind about helping.

The intercom crackled. Martha said, "It's a golden day at the Golden Glen. How may I assist you?"

Raymie heard Beverly snort.

"How may I assist you?" asked Martha again.

"Martha?" said Raymie. "It's me, um, Raymie. Raymie Clarke. I visited Isabelle a couple of days ago, and I was going to do a good deed?" A wave of dizziness washed over Raymie. She remembered the letter of complaint she had written for Isabelle. Would Martha know that she was the one who had written it? Would she hold it against her? Would she understand that Raymie had just been trying to do a good deed? Why was everything so complicated? Why were good deeds such murky things?

"Oh, Raymie, yes," said Martha's crackly voice. "Of course, of course. Isabelle will be delighted to see you again."

Raymie didn't think that this was necessarily true.

"We're here, too!" shouted Louisiana into the intercom. "We're the Three Rancheros, and we're going to—"

Beverly put her hand over Louisiana's mouth.

The door buzzed, and Raymie pulled it open. Beverly took her hand off Louisiana's mouth, and the three of them walked into the Golden Glen, where Martha was standing, like before, behind the counter at the end of the hallway, smiling.

Raymie was glad to see her.

She thought that when you died, if there was someone waiting to greet you in heaven, then that person would probably, hopefully, look like Martha — smiling, forgiving, golden, and with a blue, fuzzy sweater draped over her shoulders.

"Oh," said Martha. "You brought friends."

"We're the Three Rancheros!" said Louisiana. "We're here to right a wrong."

"Please, please —" said Beverly.

"What a lovely dress," said Martha to Louisiana.

"Thank you," said Louisiana. She twirled around so that her sleeves floated out and the sequins sparkled. "My granny made it. She makes all my dresses. She used to make the costumes for my parents, who were the Flying Elefantes."

"Isn't that interesting?" said Martha. "And I wonder what happened to your face," she said, turning to Beverly.

"It's just a bruise," said Beverly in an extremely polite voice. "From a fight. I'm okay."

"Well, then," said Martha. "As long as you

are okay. If the three of you would like to come with me." She took Louisiana's hand. "We will go upstairs and see who would like a good deed done today. Visitors are always welcome here at the Golden Glen."

Beverly rolled her eyes at Raymie, but she turned and followed Martha and Louisiana up the stairs.

Raymie walked behind Beverly. Right at the bottom of the stairs, right before she started to climb, Raymie was struck with a sudden, piercing moment of disbelief. How had she, Raymie Clarke, gotten here? At the Golden Glen? Walking behind Martha and Louisiana and Beverly — people she hadn't even known until a few days ago?

Raymie looked down at the steps. Each step was lined with a dark strip, to stop people from slipping.

"We're all baton twirlers," she heard Louisiana say to Martha. "And we're all going to compete in the Little Miss Central Florida Tire 1975 contest."

"Fascinating," said Martha.

Beverly snorted.

Raymie flexed her toes. She reminded herself of what she was doing. She was working to get the book back, to do a good deed, to win the contest, to bring her father home. She put her foot on the first dark nonstick strip and then the next one and the next.

She climbed the stairs.

Twenty-one

The common room was entirely empty. The floor was shining, but in an ordinary kind of way. The piano was silent. There were several scraggly ferns hanging from the ceiling and an unfinished jigsaw puzzle on a small table in the center of the room. The box of the puzzle was propped up to show what the picture would be when the puzzle was done: a covered bridge in autumn.

"Well," said Martha, "I have to return to my station. Maybe you three would like to take it from here and go down to Isabelle's room and knock on her door and see if she would like visitors."

"Okay," said Raymie.

"Thank you very much," said Beverly in the same terrifyingly polite voice she had used before.

"I like this room," said Louisiana. "You could dance on this floor. You could put on a show here."

"Well," said Martha, "I suppose you could. There's not a lot of dancing here, and I don't believe that we have ever had a show. But perhaps someday. Who knows?" Martha shook her head. And then she clapped her hands. "Okay, girls. You just head down the hallway. Raymie, you know which door is Isabelle's."

Raymie nodded. She knew which door was Alice Nebbley's. That was what mattered.

"Right," said Beverly when Martha was gone. "Which room?"

"It's this way," said Raymie. Beverly and Louisiana followed her down the hallway, and as they got closer, they heard it.

"Take my hand!" screamed Alice Nebbley.

"Oh, my goodness," said Louisiana. "Let's go back. Let's not do it."

"Shut up," said Beverly.

Louisiana caught up to Raymie and took her hand, and Raymie had the strange thought that holding on to Louisiana's hand was like holding the paw of one of the ghost bunnies on her barrettes. She almost wasn't even there.

But still, it was comforting for some reason, to have Louisiana's hand in hers.

"Take my hand!" shouted Alice Nebbley again.

"Just get out of the way," said Beverly. She pushed past Raymie and Louisiana and marched right into Alice Nebbley's room without knocking. Raymie could see that the room was dark, as it had been before, as dark as a cave, as dark as the grave.

"She went into the room," said Louisiana to Raymie.

"Yes," said Raymie. "She did."

They stood together in the hallway and stared

at the dark outline that was Beverly Tapinski. She was standing right next to the bed.

"Arrrgggghh!" screamed Alice Nebbley, and both Louisiana and Raymie jumped.

"It's under the bed," called Raymie.

"I know that," said Beverly from inside the darkness. "You told me that a thousand times. If there's one thing I know, it's where the stupid book is supposed to be."

Raymie saw the dark form of Beverly duck down and disappear.

"There's no book under here," said Beverly's muffled voice a minute later.

"There has to be," said Raymie.

"It's not there," said Beverly. Her shadowy form reappeared. "It's not anywhere in here. I don't know. Who knows what old people do with books. Maybe she ate it. Or is lying on top of it."

And then, instead of coming back out of the room, Beverly moved closer to Alice Nebbley's bed.

"Never mind," called Raymie. "Leave it alone. Come back." She was suddenly afraid that Beverly might do something drastic and unpredictable, like try to pick up Alice Nebbley and look underneath her.

"Arrrrggghhhhh!" screamed Alice Nebbley. "I cannot. I cannot. I cannot stand the pain."

"Oh, no," said Louisiana. "It's too terrible. She can't stand the pain. I can't stand the pain of her not standing the pain." She squeezed Raymie's hand so hard that it hurt.

"Take my hand!" screamed Alice Nebbley.

And then, just like before, a skinny arm came out from underneath the covers as if it were emerging from a grave. Louisiana screamed and Raymie let out a whimper, and in Alice Nebbley's dark and tragic room, Beverly stood quietly without jumping or moving at all. And then, slowly, she reached out and took hold of the hand.

"Ooooooohh," said Louisiana. "She took the hand. Now that woman is going to pull Beverly into the grave. She is going to kill her and use her to fashion a new soul."

Raymie had not imagined any of these

gruesome outcomes in particular, but she did feel a very deep sense of dread.

"No, no," said Louisiana. "I can't stand and watch." She dropped Raymie's hand. "I'm going to go and find someone to help."

"Don't," said Raymie.

But Louisiana was gone, running down the hallway, her sequined dress glowing and glittering in a purposeful way.

Raymie stood alone, watching as Beverly, still holding Alice Nebbley's hand, sat down on the bed.

"Shhh," said Beverly.

Alice Nebbley stopped screaming.

"It will be okay," said Beverly. And then, incredibly, she started to hum.

What was Beverly Tapinski—the safecracker, the lock picker, the gravel beater—doing sitting on Alice Nebbley's bed, holding her hand, telling her it would be okay, and humming to her?

It didn't seem possible.

And then Louisiana was standing next to Raymie again. Her small chest was rising and falling. A wheezy sound was issuing from her lungs. "I found it," she said.

"What?" said Raymie.

"I found it. I found your Florence Whatsit book."

"Nightingale," said Raymie.

"Yes," said Louisiana. "Nightingale. Nightingale. It's in the janitor's office. I went in there to see if the janitor would help Beverly fight the goblin, and then surprise! I found the book! Also, I let the bird go."

"What bird?" said Raymie.

"That little yellow bird. In the cage in the janitor's office."

At this point, someone somewhere in the Golden Glen screamed, and it wasn't Alice Nebbley.

"I had to climb up on top of the desk to do it," said Louisiana. "And then I had to leave in a hurry, so I forgot your book. I don't think that birds should be in cages, do you?"

There was another scream and the sound of running feet.

Beverly came out of Alice Nebbley's room.

"What happened?" she said.

"I'm not sure," said Raymie.

"I found the book!" said Louisiana.

A small yellow bird came whizzing down the hallway and sailed over their heads.

"Was that a bird?" asked Beverly.

In her room, Alice Nebbley was completely silent.

Raymie hoped that she wasn't dead.

Twenty-two

The janitor came running down the hallway. His keys were jangling, and his janitor boots were making a very authoritative sound as they hit the polished floor of the Golden Glen.

The janitor had a determined look on his face. He didn't seem at all like a man who would play mournful music on the piano. His fingers were too thick. Also, he didn't look very much like someone who would own a yellow bird.

"Oooooh," said Louisiana. "Hurry. Follow me."

Louisiana led them down the hallway. "In here," she said. "Right there." She pointed at a small room with the door open. Inside the room, there was a desk, and right in the center of the desk was *A Bright and Shining Path: The Life of Florence Nightingale*.

"Is that it?" asked Beverly. "Is that your stupid library book?"

Above the desk, there was a birdcage, rocking back and forth. It was empty. The little door to the cage was open.

Something about the open door on the cage made Raymie feel sad.

At home right now, Raymie's mother was probably sitting on the couch, staring into space. Mrs. Borkowski was probably in her lawn chair in the middle of the road. And Mrs. Sylvester was surely at her desk, typing, the giant jar of candy corn in front of her trembling slightly from the hum and clatter of the electric typewriter.

And Raymie's father? Maybe he was sitting in the diner with the dental hygienist. Maybe they were both holding menus. Maybe they were thinking about what they might order.

Did her father think about her?

What if he had already forgotten her?

Those were the questions Raymie wanted to ask somebody, but there wasn't anyone to ask.

"Why are you just standing there?" said Beverly. "Are you going to get the book or not?"

"Well, my goodness," said Louisiana. "I will get the book." She ran into the janitor's office and grabbed Florence Nightingale off the desk and ran back out.

From somewhere in the Golden Glen there came another scream.

"I think we should go now," said Louisiana.

"That's a good idea," said Beverly.

And the three of them started to run.

Twenty-three

Outside, in front of the Golden Glen, Louisiana was holding the book, and Beverly was sitting on the curb, and Raymie was standing and staring at nothing at all.

"You said I wouldn't be any help," said Louisiana. "But I found the book, and I retrieved the book. And I freed the bird!"

"No one told you to free a bird," said Beverly.

"Yes," said Louisiana. "That part was extra, an extra good deed."

Raymie's heart thudded somewhere deep inside of her. Good deeds, good deeds. She was so far behind on good deeds that she did not think she would ever catch up.

"You—" said Beverly. But whatever she intended to say next was interrupted by the appearance of the Elefante station wagon. It came careening down Borton Street, emitting great clouds of black smoke.

"Look," said Raymie. This was an entirely unnecessary directive. It would have been impossible to miss seeing the car.

The station wagon pulled up to the curb and screeched to a stop. A piece of decorative wood paneling was peeling off and hanging at an odd angle. It flapped back and forth thoughtfully.

"Get in, get in!" shouted Louisiana's grandmother. "She's right behind me. There's not a moment to waste."

"Is it Marsha Jean?" said Louisiana. "Is she hot on our trail?"

"Hurry!" shouted the grandmother. "All of you."

"All of us?" asked Raymie.

"Don't just stand there!" shouted the grandmother. "Get in the car!"

"Get in the car, get in the car!" shouted Louisiana. She hopped up and down. "Hurry. Marsha Jean is hot on our trail!"

Beverly looked at Raymie. She shrugged. She walked toward the station wagon and opened the back door. "You heard her," said Beverly. She held the door open. "Hurry up. There's not a moment to waste."

"Come on!" said Louisiana. She climbed into the station wagon. Raymie got in after her, and Beverly got in last. She slammed the door shut, and it immediately popped back open.

The car accelerated so quickly that they were all thrown back against the seat. The broken door slammed shut and then opened again.

"Oh, my goodness," said Louisiana. "Here we go."

And they went.

Twenty-four

Louisiana's grandmother did not believe in stop signs, or she did not see them, or maybe she did not think that they applied to her. Whatever the reason, the Elefante station wagon went past every stop sign without stopping or even slowing down very much.

They were going very, very fast, and the car emitted a lot of noises: screeches (from the piece of loose wood siding), thumps (from the door that would not stay closed), and a cacophony of mechanical grinding noises—the overworked and desperate sounds an engine makes when it has been pushed beyond its limits.

Also, from the backseat it was not possible to see Louisiana's grandmother's head, and so it seemed as if they were being driven around by an invisible person.

It all felt like a dream.

"Don't worry," said Louisiana. "Granny is the best there is. She has outwitted Marsha Jean every single time."

Beverly snorted.

At this point, the station wagon went faster—though a moment ago, Raymie would have said that this was not possible.

Raymie looked over at Beverly and raised her eyebrows.

"We're getting the heck out of Dodge," said Beverly. She grinned, displaying a chipped front tooth. Raymie wasn't sure, but she thought that it might be the first time she had seen Beverly Tapinski really, truly smile.

Louisiana laughed. "We are!" she said. "We are leaving Dodge far behind."

From the front seat, the invisible granny laughed.

And then Raymie was laughing, too.

Something was happening to her. Her soul was getting bigger and bigger and bigger. She could feel it lifting her off the seat, almost.

"The trick with people like Marsha Jean," said Louisiana's grandmother, "is to be forever wily, to fight back, to never give up or give in."

The car went a little faster still.

Raymie understood that, technically, she should be afraid. She was in a car that was being driven too fast by a person who was invisible. Plus, the car sounded like it might fall apart at any minute.

But Louisiana was on one side of her— with her bunny barrettes and her sequins and the Florence Nightingale book in her arms; and Beverly was on the other side of her— bruised, grubby-handed, and smelling like some strange combination of motor oil and cotton candy. And there was a gigantic wind blowing into the car, and Raymie's soul was as big as it had ever been before and she felt not one bit afraid.

She turned to Beverly and said, "You held Alice Nebbley's hand."

"So what?" said Beverly. She shrugged. She grinned again. "She asked me to."

"I am so happy," said Louisiana. "All of a sudden, I'm just filled up with happiness. Should I sing, Granny?"

"Of course you should sing, darling," said her grandmother.

And so Louisiana started singing "Raindrops Keep Fallin' on My Head" in the prettiest voice Raymie had ever heard. It sounded like an angel singing. Not that Raymie had ever heard an angel sing. But still, that was the way it sounded. Raymie listened and looked out the window at the stop signs rushing by.

For some reason, even though the song wasn't a sad song, it made Raymie think of sad things. It made her think of the kitchen light in her house, the one over the stove, the one that her mother left on all night long.

It made her think of how, one time, she had come out to the kitchen in the middle of the night for a drink of water and had seen her father sitting at the table with his head in his hands. He had not seen her. And Raymie had backed up slowly and gone back to bed without saying anything to him.

What was he doing at the table, alone, with his head in his hands?

She should have said something to him.

But she had not.

Louisiana finished singing, and her grand-mother said, "It does my heart good to hear you sing, Louisiana. It makes me believe that all will be well."

"All will be well, Granny," said Louisiana. "I promise you. I'm going to win that contest, and we will be rich as Croesus."

"You are the best granddaughter an old woman could hope for. And now will you just look where we are?"

"Home!" said Louisiana.

"Yes," said her grandmother.

The car slowed down and turned off the paved road and onto a dirt road.

"We can all have some tuna fish together!" said Louisiana.

"Oh, boy," said Beverly.

And then they were at the end of the dirt road, and a gigantic house was in front of them. The front porch was sagging and the chimney was tilted to one side, as if it were considering something important. Some of the windows were boarded up.

"Come on," said Louisiana. "We're here."

"Really?" said Beverly.

"Yes," said Louisiana's grandmother. "We've outsmarted Marsha Jean, and we're home."

Twenty-five

In the kitchen, there were several towering piles of empty tuna-fish cans. The walls were painted green, and for the first time, Raymie stood face-to-face with the grandmother. It was like looking at Louisiana in a fun-house mirror. The grandmother's hair was gray and her face was wrinkled, but other than that she looked exactly like her granddaughter. She was tiny, not much taller than Louisiana, and she, too, had bunny barrettes in her hair, which was strange because you did not necessarily think that old people wore barrettes.

"Welcome, welcome," said the grandmother, spreading her arms wide. "Welcome to our humble abode."

"Yes," said Louisiana. "Welcome."

"Thank you," said Raymie.

Beverly shook her head. She wandered out of the kitchen and into the living room.

"It's such a pleasure to make the acquaintance of Louisiana's best friend," said the grandmother to Raymie.

"Me?" said Raymie.

"Oh, yes, you. It's 'Raymie this' and 'Raymie that' all the livelong day. It must be wonderful to be idolized so. Now. Just let me locate the can opener," the grandmother said, "and we will have ourselves a tuna-fish feast."

"Oh, my goodness," said Louisiana. "I love it when we have tuna-fish feasts."

"Where's the furniture?" asked Beverly. She was standing at the threshold to the kitchen.

"I beg your pardon?" said Louisiana's grandmother.

"I've been all over the house and there's no furniture."

"Well, why on earth are you going all over the house searching for furniture?"

"I—" said Beverly.

"That's exactly right," said the grandmother. "Maybe you could make yourself useful and find the can opener, since you enjoy searching for things so very much."

"Okay," said Beverly. "I mean, I guess so." She stepped into the kitchen and started opening and closing doors.

"Oh," said the grandmother. She put both hands to her head. "I just now have had a sudden recollection. The can opener is in the car."

"It's in the *car*?" said Beverly.

"Louisiana, run out there and get it for me, would you, darling? And do not return until you find it."

"Yes, Granny," said Louisiana.

Louisiana turned and left in a flash of orange and sequins and bunny barrettes. As soon as the screen door slammed shut behind her, the grand-mother turned to Beverly and Raymie and pulled a can opener out of the sleeve of her dress.

"Ta-da," she said. "My father was a magician, the most elegant and deceitful man who ever lived. I learned a few things from him that I've found to be of some use—sleights of hand, for instance, how to conceal things."

She waggled her eyebrows.

"Were Louisiana's parents really trapeze art-ists?" asked Raymie. "Were they the Flying Elefantes?"

Beverly snorted.

"The story of the Flying Elefantes is a story worth telling again and again," said the grand-mother.

"But is it true?" asked Raymie.

Louisiana's grandmother raised her left eye-brow and then her right one. She smiled.

Beverly rolled her eyes.

"What about Marsha Jean?" asked Raymie. "Is she real?"

"Marsha Jean is the ghost of what's to come. It's good to be on the lookout for those who might do you harm. I need Louisiana to be cautious. And wily. I won't always be here to protect her. She would have a very hard time if she ended up in the county home. I'm hoping that you two can keep an eye on her, that you'll protect her."

The screen door slammed.

"I looked everywhere, Granny," said Louisiana. "I can't find it."

"No worries, darling. I've located it. And now we'll feast!" The grandmother held up the can opener. She smiled.

How could Raymie protect Louisiana?

She didn't even know how to protect herself.

Twenty-six

They sat on the floor of the dining room underneath a gigantic chandelier.

"It's very pretty if we turn it on," said Louisiana. "But right now, we can't turn it on because we don't have electricity."

The lack of furniture in the room made the words they said to each other sound funny. Everything echoed and bounced.

They ate tuna fish directly out of the can, and they drank water out of little paper cups that had riddles printed in red on their sides.

"They're supposed to have the answer to the riddle on the bottom, but they made a mistake and forgot to put the answer there," said Louisiana, "and that's why we got thousands of the cups for free. Because they don't have the answer. Isn't that something?"

"Yeah," said Beverly. "That's something."

Raymie held up her paper cup and read the side of it out loud. "What has three legs, no arms, and reads the paper all day long?"

She looked at the bottom of the cup. There was nothing there.

"See?" said Louisiana. "There's no answer."

"It's a stupid question," said Beverly.

Outside, there was a flash of lightning and then a large clap of thunder. The chandelier shook.

"Ooooooh," said the grandmother. "It's going to be a big one."

"It's lucky that we're safe inside and all together," said Louisiana.

The rain started to come down in sheets, and the dining room, which was painted a deep blue, became a murky underwater kind of place. Raymie wondered if they had maybe, somehow, journeyed to a different world, the four of them together. It had been such a strange day.

"Granny?" said Louisiana.

"Yes, darling."

"I miss Archie."

"Now, don't get started on that. Remember what I said: There's no point in looking back."

"But I miss him," said Louisiana. Her lower lip trembled.

"They're taking good care of him at the Very Friendly Animal Center. I'm certain of it."

Beverly snorted.

Louisiana started to cry.

"Don't think about it, darling," said the grandmother. "Some things just do not bear thinking about. Eat your tuna fish. Ponder your riddle."

Louisiana cried harder.

Beverly put her hand on Louisiana's back. She leaned over and whispered something in her ear.

"That's true," said Louisiana. "We did succeed."

"Succeed?" said the grandmother. "What did you succeed at, exactly?"

"Look," said Beverly. "My father's a cop. I know things."

"My goodness." The grandmother sat up straighter. "How interesting. May I inquire: Is your father a police officer in our fair city?"

"No," said Beverly.

"Where, then?"

"New York City," said Beverly.

"New York City!" said Raymie. "He's not here? He's in New York City?" She couldn't believe it. Beverly's father was gone. Beverly Tapinski was fatherless, too.

Raymie stared at Beverly, and Beverly stared back at her in a very fierce kind of way.

"I'm going there, okay?" said Beverly. "Just as soon as I'm old enough, I'm moving to New York. I've already run away twice. One time, I made it all the way to Atlanta."

"Atlanta!" squeaked Louisiana.

"In the meantime," said Beverly. "I'm stuck

here. With you people. Doing stupid things like looking for library books under old people's beds."

Beverly put down her tuna-fish can and got up and walked out of the dining room.

Raymie felt her soul shrink.

"My goodness," said Louisiana's grandmother.

"I think her heart is broken," said Louisiana.

Raymie's soul shrank further.

"Beware of the brokenhearted," said the grandmother, "for they will lead you astray."

Outside, it started to rain even harder.

"That's all of us, though, Granny, isn't it?" said Louisiana over the noise of the rain. "Aren't we all brokenhearted?"

Twenty-seven

The ride back to town was not fast. They still did not bother to stop for stop signs, but they went past them slowly. And there was no singing. Beverly sat with her arms crossed over her chest, Louisiana looked out the window, and Raymie stared down at *A Bright and Shining Path: The Life of Florence Nightingale* and flexed her toes. But she didn't really know what her objectives were anymore.

She was too sad for objectives.

"Don't forget," said Louisiana when Raymie got out of the car. "We succeeded, but there's another wrong that still needs to be righted."

Raymie looked down at the book in her hand.

"Okay," she said. "I'll see you Monday, at Ida Nee's."

"Yes, you will," said Louisiana. "The Rancheros will ride again. I promise you."

Beverly sat very still, her arms crossed over her chest. She didn't look at Raymie. She didn't say anything at all.

Raymie closed the door to the station wagon as quietly as she could and climbed the front steps to her house. Before she went inside, she turned and watched the car go up the street. There was black smoke pouring out of the exhaust pipe. Raymie stared at the smoke, willing it to shape itself into something that had meaning—a letter, a promise. She stared until the car disappeared.

"Where in the world have you been?" said her mother. She was holding open the front door. Behind her was the bookcase, filled with all of

Raymie's father's books, and behind that was the yellow expanse of the shag carpet, which seemed to go on forever.

"I was—" said Raymie. "I was, um, reading to the elderly."

"Come inside," said her mother. "Something has happened."

"What?" said Raymie. "What happened?" She felt her soul form itself into a small, frightened ball.

"Mrs. Borkowski," said her mother.

"Mrs. Borkowski," repeated Raymie.

She held Florence Nightingale very close to her chest, as if the lady with the lamp could protect her from whatever it was that her mother was getting ready to say.

"Mrs. Borkowski is dead."

Twenty-eight

Raymie stared at the yellow carpet. She stared at the bookcase. She couldn't look at her mother's face. She felt, more than anything else, bewildered. How could Mrs. Borkowski be dead?

"There's no funeral," said her mother. "But there will be a memorial service tomorrow at the Finch Auditorium. Mrs. Borkowski's daughter is taking care of things, and that's what she said her mother wanted: a memorial service, no funeral. Who knows why." Raymie's mother sighed. "Mrs. Borkowski was always so strange."

"But how can she be dead?" said Raymie.

"She was old," said Raymie's mother. "She had a heart attack."

"Oh."

Raymie went into the kitchen. She picked up the phone and called Clarke Family Insurance. The phone rang. Raymie looked up at the sunburst clock on the kitchen wall. The clock said that it was 5:15. Sometimes Mrs. Sylvester stayed late on Saturdays, typing things up.

The phone rang again.

"Please," said Raymie. She tried to flex her toes. But her feet were frozen, numb. Her toes wouldn't move at all.

Mr. Staphopoulos had never said what you should do if you *couldn't* flex your toes.

The phone rang a third time.

Mrs. Borkowski was dead!

"Clarke Family Insurance," said Mrs. Sylvester in her cartoon-bird voice. "How may we protect you?"

Raymie said nothing.

"Hello?" said Mrs. Sylvester.

Raymie couldn't speak.

"Is this Raymie Clarke?" asked Mrs. Sylvester.

Raymie stood in the kitchen and nodded her head. She held on to the phone and stared at the sunburst clock and thought about Mrs. Sylvester's gigantic jar of candy corn. It was so bright. It was as if it held light instead of candy corn. It was a very comforting thing to think about — a jar filled with light.

"I—" said Raymie. But she couldn't get any further than that. The sentence she needed to say was jammed up inside of her. Maybe the words were somewhere in her toes? Also, her soul felt incredibly small. She wasn't even sure where it was. She searched around inside of herself, trying to locate it.

"There, there," said Mrs. Sylvester.

"Um," said Raymie.

"He'll come back, honey," said Mrs. Sylvester.

Raymie realized that Mrs. Sylvester thought that she was upset about her father leaving.

Mrs. Sylvester didn't know that Mrs. Borkowski was dead.

Something about this made Raymie's soul even smaller and her toes even stiffer. It occurred to her that nobody really knew what anybody else was upset about, and that seemed like a terrible thing.

She missed Louisiana. She missed Beverly Tapinski.

She had another terrible thought: Where had Mrs. Borkowski's soul gone?

Where was it?

Raymie closed her eyes and saw a gigantic seabird fly by: its wings were massive — huge and dark. They didn't look like angel wings at all.

"Mrs. Borkowski?" she whispered.

"What's that, honey?" said Mrs. Sylvester.

"Mrs. Borkowski," said Raymie, louder.

"I don't know who Mrs. Borkowski is, dear," said Mrs. Sylvester. "This is Mrs. Sylvester. And everything is going to be fine, just fine."

"Okay," said Raymie.

Suddenly, it was hard to breathe.

Mrs. Borkowski was dead.

Mrs. Borkowski was dead!

Phhhhtttt.

Raymie's mother did not talk on the way to the memorial service. She sat behind the wheel of the car exactly the same way she sat on the couch, staring straight ahead, grim-faced.

The sun was shining very brightly, but the whole world looked gray, as if everything had faded overnight.

They drove past Central Florida Tire. There was a gigantic banner in the window of the store that said, "YOU could become Little Miss Central Florida Tire 1975!"

Raymie read the words and was alarmed to discover that they didn't make any sense to her.

Become Little Miss Central Florida Tire? What did that mean? The words promised her nothing.

Raymie looked down at Florence Nightingale.

She had brought the book with her because it hadn't seemed like a good idea to leave it behind.

"What's with the book?" said her mother, still staring straight ahead.

"It's a library book," said Raymie.

"Uh-huh."

"It's about Florence Nightingale. She was a nurse. She walked a bright and shining path."

"Good for her."

Raymie looked down at the book. She stared at Florence Nightingale's lamp. She was holding it up high over her head. It almost looked like she was carrying a star.

"Do you think that if you were in a deep hole in the ground and it was daylight and you looked up out of the deep hole, at the sky, you could see stars, even though it was daylight and the sun was out?"

"What?" said her mother. "No. What are you talking about?"

Raymie didn't know if she believed it either,

but she wanted to believe it. She wanted it to be true.

"Never mind," she said to her mother. And they drove the rest of the way to the Finch Auditorium in silence.

Twenty-nine

The Finch Auditorium floor was composed of green and white tiles. For as long as she could remember, Raymie had walked only on the green tiles. Someone had told her that stepping on the white ones was bad luck. Who? She couldn't remember.

There was a stage at the front of the auditorium. The stage had a piano on it and red velvet curtains that were always open. Raymie had never seen the curtains closed.

In the center of the auditorium, there was a long table. The table was covered in food, and there were people standing around it talking.

Raymie kept her right foot on a green square and her left foot on a green square and held herself very still. An adult passed by and patted her on the head.

Someone said, "I think it's mayonnaise, but I'm not sure. It's hard to tell at these things."

Someone else said, "She was a very interesting woman."

Somebody laughed. And Raymie realized that she would never hear Mrs. Borkowski laugh again.

Raymie's father had always said that Mrs. Borkowski's laugh sounded like a horse in distress. But Raymie liked it. She liked how Mrs. Borkowski threw back her head and opened her mouth wide and whinnied when something was funny. She liked how you could see all of her teeth when she laughed. She liked how Mrs. Borkowski smelled like mothballs. She liked how Mrs. Borkowski said "Phhhhtttt." She liked how she talked about people's souls. Nobody else Raymie had ever met talked about souls.

Raymie's mother was standing next to someone who was holding a shiny black purse close to her chest. Her mother was talking, and the woman with the shiny black purse was nodding at everything her mother said.

Raymie wanted to hear Mrs. Borkowski laugh.

She wanted to hear her say "Phhhhtttt."

Raymie didn't think that she had ever felt so lonely in her life. And then she heard someone say, "Oh, my goodness."

Raymie turned and there was Louisiana Elefante. And next to Louisiana was Louisiana's grandmother, who was wearing a fur coat even though it was summertime.

Louisiana's grandmother had a tissue in her hand, and she waved it back and forth in front of her face and said to no one in particular, "I am positively prostrate with grief."

"I'm prostrate with grief, too," said Louisiana. She was staring at the table full of food.

Both Louisiana and her grandmother had lots of bunny barrettes in their hair.

Louisiana.

Louisiana Elefante.

Raymie had never been so glad to see anyone in her life. "Louisiana," she whispered.

"Raymie!" shouted Louisiana. She smiled a very big smile and opened her arms wide, and Raymie walked toward her, stepping on both white tiles and green tiles. She didn't care anymore. She stepped on all the tiles because bad things happened all the time, no matter what color tile you stepped on.

Louisiana put her arms around Raymie.

Raymie let go of Florence Nightingale. The book hit the floor and made a sound like someone clapping their hands together.

Raymie started to cry. "Mrs. Borkowski is dead," she said. "Mrs. Borkowski is dead."

Thirty

"Shhhh," said Louisiana. She patted Raymie on the back. "I'm so sorry for your loss. That's what you're supposed to say at funeral gatherings. And it's true, too. I'm sorry for your loss."

Raymie heard the squeaky sound of air entering and exiting Louisiana's swampy lungs.

"I like the words 'I'm sorry for your loss,'" said Louisiana, still holding on to Raymie. "I think that they are good words. You could say them to anyone at any time. Why, you could say them to me, and it would apply to Archie or to my parents."

Raymie hiccuped. "I'm sorry for your loss," she repeated.

"There, there," said Louisiana. "You just keep crying." Her lungs squeaked and her bunny barrettes made clicking sounds each time she patted Raymie's back.

Up on the stage, someone started to play "Chopsticks" on the piano.

Raymie would have thought that there would be no comfort to be had from someone as insubstantial as Louisiana holding her, but it was actually very comforting, even with all the barrette clicking and lung wheezing.

Raymie held tight to Louisiana. She hiccuped a second time. She closed her eyes and opened them again. She saw Louisiana's grandmother standing at the food table with a gigantic bunch of green grapes in her hand. She watched as the grandmother slid the grapes into her purse. And then Louisiana's grandmother put a handful of crackers in the pocket of her fur coat.

Louisiana's grandmother was stealing food from Mrs. Borkowski's memorial food table!

The piano playing got louder. Raymie held on to Louisiana and looked around the room. Her mother was standing in a corner with her arms folded. She was listening to someone talk. She was nodding her head.

Louisiana's grandmother put an entire block of orange cheese into her purse.

Raymie felt dizzy.

"I feel dizzy," she said.

Louisiana let go of Raymie. She bent down and picked Florence Nightingale up off the floor. "Come here," she said. And she led Raymie by the hand to the stage and pushed aside one of the red curtains. A galaxy of dust rose up into the air and floated around their heads. The dust looked as if it were celebrating something.

"Now, sit down," said Louisiana. She pointed at the stage steps. Raymie sat. "You just tell me everything you know about Mrs. Boralucky."

"Borkowski," said Raymie.

"That too," said Louisiana. "Tell me."

Raymie looked down at her hands.

She tried to flex her toes, but they still wouldn't work.

"Um," she said. "Her name was Mrs. Borkowski. She lived across the street from us, and when she laughed, you could see all the teeth in her mouth."

"That's nice," said Louisiana. She patted Raymie's hand. "How many teeth did she have?"

"A lot," said Raymie. "All of them, I guess. I cut her toenails for her because she couldn't reach her feet. She paid me in divinity."

"What's divinity?" asked Louisiana.

"It's candy. It kind of looks like a cloud, and it doesn't taste like anything. It's just really, really sweet. Sometimes Mrs. Borkowski put walnuts on top of it."

"It sounds wonderful," said Louisiana. She sighed. "I'm very fond of sugar. And I think it's a good idea to put nuts on top of things, don't you?"

"Mrs. Borkowski knew the answer to everything," said Raymie.

"Well, that is just like Granny. She knows the answer to everything, too." Louisiana pulled on the velvet curtain, and another galaxy of dust rose up and swirled around them.

Raymie stared at the dancing particles.

"Phhhhtttt," she heard Mrs. Borkowski say, even though Mrs. Borkowski was dead.

And then Raymie thought: What if every piece of dust was a planet, and what if every planet was full of people, and what if all the people on all the planets had souls and were just like Raymie — trying to flex their toes and make sense out of things and not really succeeding very much?

It was a terrifying thought.

"I'm so hungry," said Louisiana. "I'm hungry all the time. Granny says that I'm a bottomless pit. She says that I'm going to eat us out of house and home. And that's why I have to win the Little

Miss Central Florida Tire 1975 contest, so that we won't starve."

"My father left," said Raymie.

"What did you say?" said Louisiana.

"My father is gone."

"But where did he go?" said Louisiana. She looked around the Finch Auditorium as if Raymie's father were there somewhere — hiding under a table or behind a curtain.

"He ran away with a dental hygienist," said Raymie.

"That's the person who cleans your teeth," said Louisiana.

"Yes," said Raymie.

Louisiana patted Raymie on the back. "I'm sorry," she said. "I'm so sorry for your loss."

"I was going to try and get him back," said Raymie. "I was going to try and win the contest and get my picture in the paper, and I thought that would bring him back."

"It would be nice to get your picture in the paper," said Louisiana. "He would be proud of you."

"I don't think that it will work," said Raymie. "I don't think any of it will work."

Just as she said these terrible words, a scuffle erupted around the food table.

Raymie heard Louisiana's grandmother shout, "Unhand me, sir!"

"Hey, now," said someone else. "Let's just stay calm."

"Uh-oh," said Louisiana.

And then Louisiana's grandmother said, "I am uncertain exactly what you are implying, but I can assure you that I do not care for the implication, whatever it is." And then she said in an even louder voice, "Louisiana! The time has come for us to depart."

"I think I have to go," said Louisiana.

She stood up and patted Raymie on the back, and then she looked her in the eye and said, "I want to tell you something."

"Okay," said Raymie.

"I am very glad to know you," said Louisiana.

"I'm glad to know you, too," said Raymie.

"And I wanted to tell you that no matter what, I'm here and you're here and we're here together." Louisiana waved her left arm through the air as if she were doing a magic trick and had just conjured up the whole of the Finch—the velvet curtains and the old piano and the green-and-white-tiled floor.

"Okay," said Raymie. She flexed her toes. Her feet felt slightly less numb.

"I'll see you tomorrow at baton-twirling lessons," said Louisiana. "But in the meantime, I think that I'll just leave out this back door. If you see Marsha Jean or the cops, don't tell them my whereabouts."

And then before Raymie could tell her not to, Louisiana went out the door marked EMERGENCY EXIT ONLY. ALARM WILL SOUND.

The alarm went off immediately.

It was very loud.

Raymie watched everyone running around the Finch trying to figure out what the emergency was. She reached up and tugged on the curtain and studied the dust as it rose up in the air and swirled and swooped.

She flexed her toes again.

She could feel her soul. It was a tiny little spark somewhere deep inside of her.

It was glowing.

Thirty-one

The world went on.

People left and people died and people went to memorial services and put orange blocks of cheese into their purses. People confessed to you that they were hungry all the time. And then you got up in the morning and pretended that none of it had happened.

You took your baton to baton-twirling lessons and stood under Ida Nee's whispering pine trees in front of Lake Clara, where Clara Wingtip had drowned. You waited with Louisiana Elefante and

Beverly Tapinski for Ida Nee to show up and teach you how to twirl a baton.

The world — unbelievably, inexplicably — went on.

"She's late," said Beverly.

"Oh, my goodness," said Louisiana. "I'm starting to worry that I'll never learn how to twirl a baton."

"Baton twirling is stupid," said Beverly. "No one needs to learn how to twirl a baton."

"I do," said Louisiana. "That's exactly what I need to know."

Raymie said nothing. It was so hot. She stared at the lake. She didn't know what she needed anymore.

"I have an idea," said Louisiana. "Let's go find Ida Nee."

"Let's not and say we did," said Beverly. She threw her baton up in the air and caught it with an elegant twist of her wrist. The bruise on her face had faded to a yellow stain. She was chewing sour-apple gum. Raymie could smell it.

"Well, I'm going to go find her," said Louisiana, "because I desperately need to win the contest and earn the money and stay out of the county home."

"Yeah," said Beverly. "Right. We know all of that already."

"Are you coming with me?" asked Louisiana.

When no one answered her, she turned away from them and headed toward the house.

Beverly looked at Raymie and shrugged.

Raymie shrugged back. And then she turned and followed Louisiana.

"Okay, okay," said Beverly. "If you say so. Besides, it's not like there's anything else to do."

The three of them walked up to Ida Nee's gravel driveway.

"We're the Three Rancheros," said Louisiana, "and we're going on a search-and-rescue mission."

"You tell yourself whatever story you want to tell yourself," said Beverly.

When they got to the driveway, they stopped and stood together and surveyed the house and garage. Everything was quiet. Ida Nee was nowhere in sight.

"Maybe she's in her office," said Louisiana, "planning out what to teach us next."

"Yeah, right," said Beverly.

Louisiana knocked on the garage door. Nothing happened. Beverly came up behind Louisiana and reached around her and jiggled the doorknob.

"This lock is no problem," said Beverly. She took her pocketknife out of her shorts and passed her baton to Raymie. "Hold this," she said.

She went to work on the lock. She got a thoughtful look on her face.

"Um," said Raymie, "should we be breaking into Ida Nee's office?"

"What else is there to do?" said Beverly.

She fiddled with the lock for a few more seconds and then smiled a big smile. "There," she said.

The door swung wide.

"Oh, my goodness," said Louisiana. "That's a very good skill to have."

"It beats baton twirling," said Beverly.

Louisiana peered into the office. "Miss Nee?" she said. "We're here for our baton-twirling lesson?"

Beverly gave Louisiana a little shove. "If you want to find her so much, go inside."

"Miss Nee?" said Louisiana again. She stepped farther into the office. Beverly and Raymie followed her. The floor and the walls of the garage were covered in green shag carpet. The ceiling was green-shag-carpeted, too. Baton-twirling trophies were everywhere, hundreds and hundreds of them gleaming in the green dimness so that the garage looked like the cave of Ali Baba. Against the far wall, there was a desk with a nameplate on it. The nameplate read IDA NEE, STATE CHAMPION.

Above the desk, there was a moose head.

"Boy, if there was ever a place that needed to be sabotaged," said Beverly, "this is it. Ida Nee acts like she's champion of everything. But some of these trophies aren't even hers. See this one?" She pointed. "This one belongs to my mother."

Louisiana squinted at the trophy. "It says Rhonda Joy," she said. "Who's Rhonda Joy?"

"That was my mother's name. Before she married my father."

"You could have been Beverly Joy!" said Louisiana.

"No," said Beverly. "I couldn't have."

"Your mother was a baton twirler?" said Raymie.

"My mother was a baton twirler and a beauty queen," said Beverly. "But who cares? Now she's not either one of those things. Now she's just someone who works in the Belknap Tower gift shop selling canned sunshine and rubber alligators."

"There's a king's ransom in here," said Louisiana. "We could sell all these trophies and never have to worry about money again."

"These things are nothing but junk," said Beverly.

Raymie was listening to Beverly and Louisiana

and also not listening to them. She was staring up at the moose head, and he was staring back at her.

The moose had the saddest eyes of anyone she had ever seen.

They looked like Mrs. Borkowski's eyes.

One time, when Raymie was cutting Mrs. Borkowski's toenails, Mrs. Borkowski had asked Raymie a question. She had said, "Tell me, why does the world exist?"

And Raymie had looked up at Mrs. Borkowski's face, into her sad eyes, and said, "I don't know."

"Exactly," said Mrs. Borkowski. "You don't know. No one knows. No one knows."

"What are you staring at?" said Beverly.

"Nothing," said Raymie. "It's just that the moose looks sad."

"He's dead," said Beverly. "Of course he's sad."

"But let's not lose sight of the real problem," said Louisiana, "which is that Ida Nee is missing."

"Duh," said Beverly.

"Maybe we should look in the house," said Louisiana.

Raymie stared at the moose.

Phhhhtttt. Tell me, why does the world exist?

"Come on," said Beverly. "You have to keep moving." She put her hand on Raymie's shoulder and turned her around, back toward the door, where the light from the outside world was coming in.

Raymie blinked.

"Just keep moving," said Beverly again.

And Raymie walked toward the open door.

Thirty-two

They knocked on the front door of Ida Nee's house and rang the doorbell, and when no one answered, Louisiana said, "Maybe she needs help. Maybe the Three Rancheros should come to her rescue."

"Ha," said Beverly.

"Maybe you should break and enter," said Louisiana.

"Now, there's an idea," said Beverly. And she got out her pocketknife and picked the lock on Ida Nee's front door.

"Miss Nee?" shouted Louisiana. "It's us, the Three Rancheros."

From somewhere deep inside the house, there came the sound of singing and also the sound of snoring.

Louisiana went around the corner first. Beverly followed her. Raymie followed Beverly.

"She's asleep," whispered Louisiana, turning back to them. "Look!" She pointed at Ida Nee, who was stretched out on a plaid couch. One arm was hanging almost to the floor, and with the other arm, she was holding her baton close to her chest. She had on her white boots.

There was a country music song playing on the radio. It was somebody singing about how somebody else was leaving. So many country-western songs seemed to be about people leaving other people.

Ida Nee's mouth was hanging open.

"She looks just like a sleeping princess in a fairy tale," said Louisiana.

"She looks like she's drunk," said Beverly. She bent over and tickled the top of Ida Nee's arm.

"Oh, my goodness," said Louisiana. "Don't do that. Don't make her angry." Louisiana bent down close to Ida Nee's ear. She said, "Rise and shine, Miss Nee. It's lesson time."

Nothing happened.

Raymie looked at Ida Nee and then she looked away. There was something scary about watching an adult sleep. It was as if no one at all were in charge of the world. Raymie stared, instead, at Lake Clara. The lake was blue and sparkling.

Clara Wingtip had sat in front of her cabin for thirty-six straight days, waiting for her husband to return from the Civil War. And then on the thirty-seventh day, she went and drowned herself in the lake. By mistake. Or on purpose. Who could say how it had happened?

On the thirty-eighth day, David Wingtip had returned.

But it was too late. It didn't matter. Clara was already gone.

How long are you supposed to wait? That was another question that Raymie wished she had asked Mrs. Borkowski. How long should you wait, and when should you stop waiting?

Maybe, thought Raymie, *I should go out to the garage and ask the moose head that question.*

Tell me, why does the world exist?

"I'm going to take her baton," said Beverly.

"What?" said Raymie.

"I'm going to take her baton. Watch."

"No, no, no," said Louisiana. She put her hands over her eyes. "Don't do it. I can't watch."

Beverly leaned over the sleeping Ida Nee. The world became very quiet. The song on the radio ended. Ida Nee stopped snoring.

"Oh, no," said Louisiana from behind her hands.

"Please," said Raymie.

"Don't be such big babies," said Beverly. She bent over Ida Nee, and the baton became a silver rope running through Beverly's fingers. "Ta-da!" said Beverly. She stood up. She held out the baton. It flashed in the light shining off of Lake Clara.

"Oh, my goodness," said Louisiana.

Beverly threw the baton up in the air and caught it. "Sabotage!" she said. "Sabotage, sabotage!"

Another country music song came on the radio. Ida Nee snorted once, twice. And then she started to snore again.

Beverly threw the baton up in the air, higher this time. She twirled it behind her back. She twirled it in front of her, so fast and furious that the baton became almost invisible.

"Oh," said Louisiana, "you're a genius at twirling."

"I'm a genius at everything," said Beverly. She kept twirling. She smiled, revealing her chipped front tooth. "Come on," she said. "Let's get out of here."

And they did.

Thirty-three

They left Ida Nee's and started walking down Lake Clara Road, back toward town. Raymie was carrying Beverly's baton and her own baton.

Beverly stopped occasionally to beat Ida Nee's baton against the small rocks and gravel on the side of the road. The lake glinted, appearing and then disappearing again, as the road curved and they walked farther and farther away.

"Where are we going?" asked Raymie.

"We're getting the heck out of Dodge," said Louisiana.

"That's right," said Beverly. She stopped and beat some more gravel with Ida Nee's baton. "Getting. The heck. Out."

"I know what," said Louisiana.

"What?" said Raymie.

"It's time. We Three Rancheros should go and rescue Archie."

"We're not the Three Rancheros," said Beverly.

"Well, who are we, then?" asked Louisiana.

"Look," said Beverly. "That cat can't be rescued."

"You said you would help. Let's just go to the Very Friendly Animal Center and ask for him."

"There is no Very Friendly Animal Center!" shouted Beverly. "How many times do I have to tell you that?"

Raymie stood between Beverly and Louisiana and flexed her toes. She was suddenly terrified.

"Are you going to help me or not?" said Louisiana. She stared at Beverly and Raymie. Her bunny barrettes glowed a molten pink on her head.

It was so hot.

"Fine," said Beverly. "We can go and look for the cat. All I'm saying is that you don't understand how the world works."

"I do so understand how the world works," said Louisiana. She stamped her foot on the gravel. "I know exactly how it works. My parents drowned! I am an orphan! There is nothing to eat at the county home except for bologna sandwiches! And that is one way the world works."

Louisiana took a deep breath. Raymie heard her lungs wheeze.

"Your father is in New York City," said Louisiana. She pointed at Beverly. "And you tried to get to him, but you couldn't. You only made it to Georgia, and Georgia is just the next state up. That's not far away at all. And *that's* how the world works."

Louisiana's face was very red. Her bunny barrettes were on fire. "And your father," she said, twirling to face Raymie, "has run away with a tooth-cleaning person, and you don't know if he'll ever come back. And that's how the world works!

But Archie is King of the Cats, and I betrayed him. I want him back, and I want you to help me because we're friends. And that's also how the world works."

Louisiana stamped her foot one more time. A little cloud of gravel dust rose up between the three of them.

Raymie could feel her soul somewhere deep inside of her. It was a small, sad, heavy thing, a tiny marble made out of lead. She knew, suddenly, that she wasn't going to become Little Miss Central Florida Tire. She wasn't even going to try to become Little Miss Central Florida Tire.

But Louisiana was her friend, and Louisiana needed to be protected, and the only thing Raymie could think to do to make things better right now was to be a good Ranchero.

And so Raymie said, "I'll go with you to the Very Friendly Animal Center, Louisiana. I'll help you get Archie back."

The sun was high, high above them. It was beating down on them, staring, waiting.

"Fine," said Beverly. She shrugged. "If that's what we're doing, then that's what we're doing."

They walked the rest of the way into town in silence.

Louisiana led them.

Thirty-four

The Very Friendly Animal Center was a building made out of cinder blocks that were painted gray. Once, maybe in some other, happier time, the cinder blocks had been pink. In several places, the gray was peeling away to reveal the pink, so it looked like the Very Friendly Animal Center had a skin disease.

There was a small sign on the door. It said BUILDING 10.

The door was made out of warped wood painted gray.

There was one small tree cringing in front of the building. It was leafless and brown.

"This is it?" said Beverly. "This is the place?"

"It says it's Building Ten," said Raymie.

"This is the Very Friendly Animal Center. This is where Granny brought Archie." Louisiana's voice was high and tight.

"Okay, okay," said Beverly. "Fine. This is the place. Do me a favor and let me do the talking, okay? Keep your mouth shut for once."

It was very dark inside Building 10. There was a metal desk and a metal filing cabinet and a single lightbulb hanging from the ceiling. The floors were cement. There was a woman sitting at the desk eating a sandwich. And there was a door that was closed and that led to who knew where.

Each of these details emerged out of the gloom slowly, grudgingly.

"Yep?" said the woman at the desk.

"We're here to pick up a cat," said Beverly.

"No cats," said the woman. "We put the cats down the day they come in."

"Oh, no," said Raymie.

The woman took a bite out of her sandwich.

"Put them down?" said Louisiana. "Put them down where? Put them down what? A chute?"

The woman didn't answer. She sat and studied her sandwich.

From behind the closed door, there came a terrible noise. It was a howl of desperation and need and sorrow. It was the loneliest sound Raymie had ever heard. It was worse than Alice Nebbley shouting for someone to take her hand. All the hairs on the back of Raymie's neck stood up. Her soul shriveled. She grabbed hold of Louisiana's arm.

"What's behind that door?" said Louisiana. She pointed at the door with her baton.

"Nothing," said the woman.

"Look," said Beverly. "The cat's name is Archie. Can you check your records or something?"

"We don't keep records of cats," said the woman. "Too many cats. The cats come in. We put the cats down."

"Down where?" said Louisiana.

"Come on," said Beverly. "We're leaving."

"No," said Louisiana. "We're not leaving. He's my cat. I want him back."

The howl rose up again. It filled the building. The woman at the desk took another bite out of her sandwich, and the lightbulb in the center of the room swayed back and forth as if it were trying to get up enough energy to leave Building 10 and go and find another, better room to illuminate.

Raymie was still holding on to Louisiana. Beverly grabbed Louisiana's other hand. "Come on," she said. "Now. We have to leave."

"No," said Louisiana. But she let them pull her toward the door and then out the door and into the sunshine.

"What does she mean *put down?*" asked Louisiana when they were all the way outside.

"Look," said Beverly. "I told you. I've been telling you. The cat is gone."

"What do you mean gone?" said Louisiana.

"Dead," said Beverly.

Dead.

It was such a terrible word—so final, so inarguable. Raymie looked up at the blue sky, the sun.

"Maybe Archie is with Mrs. Borkowski," said Raymie to Louisiana. She had a sudden vision of Mrs. Borkowski sitting in her lawn chair in the middle of the street with a cat in her lap.

"No," said Louisiana. "You lie. Archie isn't dead. I would know if he was dead."

And then before anybody could stop her, Louisiana opened the warped wooden door and went back inside.

"Hey," said Raymie.

"Here we go," said Beverly.

They went together back into Building 10, where Louisiana was shouting. "Give him back, give him back, give him back to me!" while kicking the metal desk.

The woman with the sandwich didn't seem upset or even particularly surprised at what was happening. Louisiana stopped kicking the desk and started beating it with her baton. This seemed to unnerve the woman a tiny bit. Probably no one had ever beaten her desk with a baton before. She put down her sandwich.

"Stop that," she said.

The baton hitting the desk made a hollow, reverberating noise. It sounded like a broken drum heralding the announcement of the death of a king.

"I will stop it. Just as soon. As you give me. Back Archie!" shouted Louisiana.

Raymie thought that it was maybe the bravest thing she had ever seen, someone demanding back something that was already gone. Watching Louisiana, Raymie felt her soul lifting up inside of her, even though the entire world was dark and sad and lit only by a single lightbulb.

"You were supposed to take care of him," said Louisiana to the lady. *Bang.* "You were supposed to feed him three times a day"—*bang*—"and scratch him behind the ears"—*bang*—"just the way he likes."

Bang, bang, bang.

From behind the closed door, the terrible howl rose up again.

Louisiana stopped beating the baton against the desk. She stood and listened, and then she bent over and put her hands on her knees and started taking in big gulps of air.

"She's going to pass out now," said Beverly to Raymie. "When she does, you grab her hands and I'll grab her feet, and we'll carry her out of here."

"I am not," said Louisiana. "Going to. Pass out."

And then she toppled over sideways.

"Now," said Beverly. Raymie picked up Louisiana's hands and Beverly picked up her feet, and they carried her out of the Very Friendly Animal Center and laid her down under the small defeated tree.

Louisiana's chest was rising and falling. Her eyes were closed.

"Now what?" said Beverly.

Raymie flexed her toes. She closed her eyes and saw the single lightbulb swaying back and forth. It wasn't bright enough at all. The lightbulb was too small for that terrible dark room.

There wasn't enough light anywhere, really.

And then Raymie remembered Mrs. Sylvester's candy-corn jar. She saw it glowing in the late-afternoon sunlight streaming through the window of Clarke Family Insurance.

"We can take her to my father's office," said Raymie. "It's not far."

Thirty-five

"What is happening?" said Mrs. Sylvester in her little bird voice. "What is going on, Raymie Clarke? Why are all of you girls soaking wet? Is it raining?" Mrs. Sylvester turned her head and looked at the sun shining through the plate-glass window of Clarke Family Insurance.

"We had to take her through the sprinkler," said Beverly, "to, um, revive her enough so that she could walk here."

"Take her through the sprinkler?" said Mrs. Sylvester. "Revive her?"

"They've got Archie, and they won't give him back," said Louisiana. She raised her fist in the air and shook it. And then she said, "I feel like maybe I should sit down."

"Archie is her cat," said Raymie. "She fainted."

"Someone took your cat?" said Mrs. Sylvester.

"I really want to sit down now," said Louisiana.

"Of course, dear," said Mrs. Sylvester. "Go ahead and sit down."

Louisiana sank to the floor.

"Who took her cat?" asked Mrs. Sylvester.

"It's complicated," said Raymie.

"It smells good in here," said Louisiana in a dreamy voice.

The office smelled like pipe smoke, even though Raymie's father did not smoke a pipe and neither did Mrs. Sylvester. The man who had owned the office before, an insurance salesman named Alan Klondike, had been the pipe smoker. The smell had lingered.

"Raymie?" said Mrs. Sylvester.

"These are my friends from baton-twirling class," said Raymie.

"Isn't that sweet," said Mrs. Sylvester.

"Oh, my goodness," said Louisiana. "Is that candy corn?" She pointed at the jar on Mrs. Sylvester's desk.

"Why, yes, it is," said Mrs. Sylvester. "Would you like some?"

"I'm going to lie down for just a minute," said Louisiana, "and then when I get up, I will be ready to eat some candy corn." Louisiana went slowly from a sitting position to a lying-down position.

"Oh, dear," said Mrs. Sylvester. She wrung her hands together. "What in the world is wrong?"

"She'll be fine," said Beverly. "It's just the thing with the cat. Archie. It's got her upset. Also, her lungs are swampy."

Mrs. Sylvester raised her plucked eyebrows very high on her head. The phone rang. "Oh dear," she said.

"You should go ahead and answer the phone," said Beverly.

Mrs. Sylvester looked relieved. She picked up the phone. "Clarke Family Insurance," she said. "How may we protect you?"

The sun shone in through the plate-glass window. The window had Raymie's father's name on it—Jim Clarke—and the letters of his name made shadows on the floor.

Raymie sat down next to Louisiana on the sun-faded carpet. She felt light-headed. She didn't think that she would faint, but she felt strange, uncertain.

Beverly crouched down, too. She said to Louisiana, "Get up. You can have some candy corn if you get up."

Mrs. Sylvester was still on the phone. She said, "Mr. Clarke isn't available, but I'm sure that I can take care of that for you, Mr. Lawrence. However, right now, there is something of a situation here in the offices of Clarke Family Insurance. Would tomorrow work for you? Wonderful, wonderful. I thank you so much. Yes. Mmmmm-hmmmm. Thank you for calling."

Mrs. Sylvester hung up the phone.

Raymie closed her eyes and saw the single lightbulb from Building 10 swaying back and forth. She felt very tired. So much had happened. So much kept happening.

"I feel better," said Louisiana. She sat up. "Can I have that candy corn now?"

"Of course," said Mrs. Sylvester. She took the lid off the jar and held the jar out toward Louisiana. Louisiana stood up. She put her hand deep into the candy corn.

"Thank you," she said to Mrs. Sylvester. And then she shoved the whole handful of candy corn in her mouth. She chewed for a long time. She smiled at Mrs. Sylvester. She swallowed. She said, "Do you think there's candy corn at the county home?"

Mrs. Sylvester said, "I think that you should have some more, dear." She extended the jar again.

Raymie looked around and saw that Beverly had opened the door to her father's office and was standing and staring inside it.

Raymie got off the floor. She went and stood next to Beverly.

"This is my dad's office," she said.

"Uh-huh," said Beverly. "I figured." She was staring at the aerial photograph of Lake Clara that hung over Jim Clarke's desk.

"You can see the ghost of Clara Wingtip in that picture," said Raymie.

"Where?" said Beverly.

"Right there," said Raymie. She stepped into the office and pointed to the far right-hand side of the lake, to the dark blur that was shaped like a lost and waiting person who had drowned by mistake, or maybe on purpose.

Raymie's father had shown Clara Wingtip's ghost to her when she was six years old. He had put her on his shoulders so that she was close to the photograph, and Raymie had traced the shadow of Clara with her fingertip. For a long time after that, she had been afraid to go into his office, afraid that Clara was waiting for her and that her ghost would pull Raymie into the lake, pull her under the water and drown her somehow.

"That's just a shadow," said Beverly. "It doesn't mean anything. Shadows are all over the place. Shadows aren't ghosts."

The phone rang again. Mrs. Sylvester answered it. "Clarke Family Insurance. How may we protect you?"

"Has he called you?" said Beverly.

"Who?" asked Raymie.

"Your father," said Beverly.

"No," said Raymie.

Beverly nodded her head slowly. "Right," she said. But she didn't say it in a mean way. Raymie was standing close enough to Beverly that she could smell her, that strange combination of sweetness and grittiness. She studied the fading bruise on Beverly's face.

"Who hit you?" she asked.

"My mother," said Beverly.

"Why?"

"I shoplifted."

"Why?" asked Raymie again.

"Because," said Beverly. She put her hands in the pockets of her shorts. "I'm getting out of here. I'm going to live on my own. I'm going to take care of myself."

Behind them, Louisiana was telling Mrs. Sylvester that her parents were gone.

"They drowned," said Louisiana.

"No," said Mrs. Sylvester.

"Yes," said Louisiana.

"I'm not going to enter the Little Miss Central Florida Tire contest," said Raymie.

"Good for you," said Beverly. She nodded. "Contests are stupid."

"I don't care anymore," said Raymie.

"Sure," said Beverly. "I'm probably not going to bother doing the sabotaging, either. At least I'm not going to sabotage that contest." And then in a soft voice, she said, "I feel pretty bad about the dead cat business."

And at that point, Raymie felt everything — all of it — wash over her: Mrs. Borkowski, Archie, Alice Nebbley, the gigantic seabird, Florence Nightingale, Mr. Staphopoulos, Ida Nee's sad-eyed moose, her missing father, Clara Wingtip's ghost, the yellow bird and the empty cage, Edgar the drowning dummy, the single lightbulb in Building 10.

Tell me, why does the world exist?

Raymie took a deep breath. She stood as straight and tall as she could. She looked at the ghost of Clara Wingtip.

Which wasn't really there. Which was only a shadow.

Probably.

Thirty-six

Mrs. Sylvester held the door open for them as they left.

"Thank you for visiting," she said.

"And thank you for the candy corn," said Louisiana. "It was delicious."

On the walk back to Ida Nee's, Louisiana sang "Raindrops Keep Fallin' on My Head" twice in a row. When she started in on it a third time, Beverly told her to knock it off.

"Okay," said Louisiana. "It's just that singing helps me think. I have now made up my mind."

"Made up your mind about what?" said Raymie.

"I've decided that they're hiding Archie from me. He's behind the closed door in that place. What we need to do is break into the Very Friendly Animal Center and unlock that door. And then we'll find him. I know we will."

"What?" said Beverly. "Are you nuts? Don't you remember anything that just happened? The cat is gone. There's nobody to break in and free."

"We'll wait until it's dark," said Louisiana. "And then we'll break in and rescue him!"

"No," said Beverly.

"Yes," said Louisiana.

"The cat is dead," said Beverly.

Louisiana dropped her baton. She put her fingers in her ears. She began to hum.

Raymie bent and picked up Louisiana's baton.

"I'm not going back into that place," said Beverly.

Louisiana took her fingers out of her ears. "Why do the Rancheros even exist if they can't perform acts of bravery?"

"The Rancheros don't exist," said Beverly. "They're only in your head."

"They do exist," said Louisiana, "because we exist. We're here."

"I'm here," said Raymie.

"That's right," said Louisiana.

"And you're here," said Raymie, pointing at Louisiana. "And you're here." She pointed at Beverly. "And we're here together."

"Right," said Louisiana again.

"Duh," said Beverly. "Duh that we are all here. But none of that changes the fact that the cat is dead."

The argument went on this way for a while — Beverly insisting that the cat was dead, Louisiana insisting that they would rescue the cat — but it stopped entirely when they got to the end of Ida Nee's driveway and saw that Beverly's mother was there and Raymie's mother was there and Louisiana's grandmother was not there.

And that there was also a police car in the circular driveway.

"The cops," said Beverly.

"Oh, no," said Louisiana.

Ida Nee was standing in front of her house talking to one of the policemen. She had outfitted herself with a fresh baton, and she was using it to point at things. She pointed at the garage door. She pointed at the kitchen door.

"No!" shouted Ida Nee. "I have not lost it. I have never lost a baton in my life. It has been stolen from me. The door to my office has been jimmied. My front door has been jimmied. I am the victim of a theft."

Just when you thought that the day couldn't get any worse than Building 10 and the single lightbulb and the terrible howling and the cat killing, Ida Nee went and called the police because Beverly Tapinski had taken her baton.

They were all going to get sent to jail!

Raymie and Beverly and Louisiana were standing together at the edge of the property, right beside Ida Nee's azalea bush.

Farther up the driveway, deep inside the half

circle of it, Beverly's mother was leaning against her bright-blue car smoking a cigarette. Raymie's mother was sitting in the Clarke car, staring straight ahead.

"Oh, no," said Louisiana again.

"Let's not panic," said Beverly.

"I'm not panicking," said Louisiana.

"I think I left that stupid baton of hers at your dad's office," said Beverly.

"Oh, noooo," said Louisiana.

"Shut up," said Beverly. "They can't prove anything. We came for baton-twirling lessons and she wasn't here, so we left. That's our story. All we need to do is stick to it."

Raymie felt fuzzy, trembly. Her heart was beating very fast. Her soul, of course, had disappeared.

It was at this point that Louisiana's grandmother stuck her hand out of the azalea bush and grabbed Raymie's ankle.

Raymie screamed.

Louisiana screamed.

Beverly yelped.

Fortunately, no one heard them because Ida Nee was still pointing at things and yelling about how she had been wronged.

"Granny," said Louisiana, "what are you doing down there?"

"There's nothing to fear," whispered Louisiana's grandmother from where she was crouched in the azalea bush. She kept her hand wrapped around Raymie's ankle. Her grip was surprisingly strong.

"Don't be afraid," said the grandmother.

"Okay," said Raymie.

"I've come up with a plan." She gave Raymie's ankle a friendly little shake. "All will be well."

Raymie stared down at Louisiana's grandmother's barrette-filled, glowing head. It looked like her hair was on fire.

"Okay," said Raymie.

She was just glad that someone had a plan.

Thirty-seven

Louisiana and Raymie were in the backseat of the Clarke automobile.

They were getting the heck out of Dodge.

According to Louisiana's grandmother, the authorities were on a rampage, and it would be a good idea for Louisiana to be "far, far away from the Elefante homestead."

So Louisiana was going to spend the night at Raymie's house.

That was Louisiana's grandmother's plan.

And at midnight, Beverly Tapinski was going to come to Raymie's house, and the three of them, the Three Rancheros, were going to break into Building 10 and set free a dead cat.

That was the Rancheros' plan.

It was a plan that had been hastily concocted after Louisiana's grandmother left the scene.

It was exactly the kind of plan that Mrs. Borkowski would have approved of. Mrs. Borkowski would have laughed. She would have displayed all her teeth. And then she would have said, "Phhhhtttt, I wish you luck."

"Wasn't that exciting?" said Louisiana as they drove away from Ida Nee's. "I wonder who stole Miss Nee's baton."

She elbowed Raymie in the ribs.

"It was a tempest in a teapot," said Raymie's mother. "That's what it was. Who in the world calls the police about a missing baton?"

"I'm excited to be spending the night at your house," said Louisiana. "Is there going to be dinner, Mrs. Nightingale?"

There was a pause. "Who are you talking to?" Raymie's mother asked.

"I'm speaking to you, Mrs. Nightingale."

"My name is Mrs. Clarke."

"Oh," said Louisiana. "I didn't know. I thought that you had the same last name as Raymie."

"My last name is Clarke, too," said Raymie.

"Is it?" said Louisiana. "I thought you were Raymie Nightingale. Like the book."

"No," said Raymie. "I'm Raymie Clarke."

Where did Louisiana get such strange ideas? And what would it be like to be Raymie Nightingale? What would it be like to walk the bright and shining path and carry a lamp over your head?

"Okay," said Louisiana. "Anyway. Is there going to be dinner, Mrs. Clarke?"

"Of course there's going to be dinner."

"Oh, my goodness," said Louisiana. "What will it be?"

"Spaghetti."

"Or maybe meat loaf?" asked Louisiana. "I love meat loaf."

"I suppose I could make meat loaf," said Raymie's mother. She sighed.

Raymie looked out the window. Somewhere, her father was getting ready to eat dinner, too. She thought about him sitting in the booth at the diner with Lee Ann Dickerson, holding a menu and smoking his cigarette. She watched Lee Ann Dickerson reach forward and put her hand on her father's arm. She watched the smoke from her father's cigarette curl up to the ceiling, and suddenly she knew.

Her father was not coming back.

He was never coming back.

"Oof," said Raymie. Her soul shriveled. It felt like someone had punched her in the stomach.

"What did you say?" asked Louisiana.

"Nothing," said Raymie.

"Maybe after dinner we can read aloud from the Nightingale book," said Louisiana. "Granny always reads to me at night."

"Sure," said Raymie.

*

At dinner, Raymie's mother watched in astonishment as Louisiana consumed four entire pieces of meat loaf and all her green beans. The three of them sat at the dining-room table, underneath the small chandelier.

Louisiana said, "We have a chandelier, too. But right now we can't light it up because of the electricity issue. It's nice to have some light. Also, I like this table. This is a very big table."

"Yes," said Raymie's mother. "It is."

"You could fit a lot of people around this table," said Louisiana.

"I suppose so," said Raymie's mother.

And then they were all silent.

Raymie could hear the sunburst clock in the kitchen, ticking slowly, methodically.

"Your mother is a very good cook," said Louisiana when dinner was over and they were in Raymie's room with the door closed. "But she doesn't talk very much, does she?"

"No," said Raymie. "I guess not." She stared up at the light on the ceiling. A moth was fluttering around it hopefully.

"Did your father kiss you good night when he lived here?" asked Louisiana.

"Sometimes," said Raymie. She didn't want to think about her father anymore. She didn't want to remember him bending over and kissing her forehead or putting his hand on her shoulder. She didn't want to remember him smiling at her.

"Granny always kisses me good night," said Louisiana. "And then she gives me kisses from the absent ones. That's my mother and my father and my grandfather. I get four kisses."

Louisiana sighed. She looked out the window. "There's no one to kiss you good night in the county home. At least that's what I hear. Do you want to read aloud from the Florence Nightingale book now?"

"Okay," said Raymie.

"I'll go first," said Louisiana. She picked up

the book and opened it to the middle and read a single sentence.

"Florence was lonely."

And then she shut the book and opened it again and read a line from page three.

"Florence wanted to help."

And then she slammed the book shut.

"Shouldn't you start from the beginning?" asked Raymie.

"Why?" said Louisiana. "This way is much more interesting." She opened the book again. She read the line "Florence held up the lamp."

Outside Raymie's window, the world was dark.

"When you read a book this way," said Louisiana, "you never know what's going to happen next. It keeps you on your toes. That's what Granny says. And it's important to be on your toes because you just never know what might happen next in this world."

Thirty-eight

Raymie woke up. The hands on the Baby Ben glowed cheerily in the dark. They said that it was 1:14.

It was past midnight, and Beverly Tapinski had not shown up.

That meant that they were not going to sneak out of the house and break into Building 10 and steal Archie. Who wasn't even there.

None of it was going to happen after all. Raymie was disappointed. And relieved. Both things at the same time.

She lay in bed and stared at the clock. It ticked in a satisfied and self-important way, as if it had managed to solve some difficult problem.

Raymie got out of bed. By the orangey light of the night-light, she could see Louisiana asleep on the floor.

A Bright and Shining Path: The Life of Florence Nightingale was open on top of Louisiana's stomach. Her hands were crossed over the book, and her legs were straight out in front of her. It looked as if she had fallen on the battlefield of life.

"Fallen on the battlefield of life" was something that Louisiana had said when they were reading aloud from the book.

"Florence Nightingale helps those who have fallen on the battlefield of life. She comes to them with her magic globe—"

"I don't think it's a magic globe," said Raymie. "It's a lantern. It's what people used before electricity."

"I know that," said Louisiana. She lowered the book and stared at Raymie. She raised the book again. She said, "She comes to them with her magic globe and makes them well. They don't worry anymore. And they don't wish for things that are gone."

Raymie felt her heart thud inside of her.

"Where does it say that?" she said.

"It's written in the book in my head," said Louisiana. She tapped her head. "And that's sometimes better than the actual book. And by that, I mean that sometimes I read the words I want to be there instead of the words that are actually there. Just like Granny does." Louisiana looked up at Raymie in a very serious way. "Do you want me to keep going?"

"Yes," said Raymie.

"Good," said Louisiana. "Inside the magic globe that Florence Nightingale carries, there are wishes and hopes and love. And all of these things are very tiny and also very bright. And there are thousands of wishes and hopes and love things, and they move around in the magic globe, and that's what Florence uses to see by. That is how she sees soldiers who have fallen on the battlefield of life.

"But there comes a time when someone very evil decides to steal Florence Nightingale's magic globe, and that person's name is Marsha Jean. Florence has to fight back! And one of the things she uses is her cloak, which in the nighttime turns into a gigantic pair of wings so that Florence can fly over the battlefields with her magic globe searching for the wounded.

"But if Marsha Jean succeeds in stealing the magic globe, then Florence will be flying through darkness and won't see anything at all, and how will she help people then?"

Louisiana rustled the pages of the book.

"Do you want me to read you more?" she said.

"Yes," said Raymie.

She fell asleep while Louisiana read aloud from a book that didn't exist, and she dreamed that Mrs. Borkowski was sitting in her lawn chair in the middle of the road. And then suddenly, Mrs. Borkowski wasn't sitting in the chair. She was standing up and walking away from Raymie. She was walking down a long road, carrying a suitcase.

Raymie followed her.

"Mrs. Borkowski!" she called out in her dream.

Mrs. Borkowski stopped. She put the suitcase down on its side and opened it slowly; then she reached into the suitcase and pulled out a black cat and put him down on the ground.

"For you," said Mrs. Borkowski.

"Archie!" said Raymie. The cat twined himself through her legs. She could hear him purring.

"Yes, Archie," said Mrs. Borkowski. She smiled. And then she bent over and rummaged through the suitcase. "I have another thing for you," she said. She stood up. She was holding a globe of light.

"Wow," said Raymie.

"You hold it," said Mrs. Borkowski. She handed the globe to Raymie, and then closed the suitcase and picked it up and walked away.

"Wait," said Raymie.

But Mrs. Borkowski was already very far away.

Raymie held the magic globe up as high as

she could. She watched Mrs. Borkowski until she disappeared.

"Meow?" said Archie.

Raymie looked down at the cat. She thought, *Louisiana will be so happy. She was right. Archie isn't dead.*

That was the dream.

Raymie remembered it as she stood and considered the sleeping Louisiana. She could hear her lungs wheezing; she looked very small.

Suddenly, without any warning at all, Louisiana opened her eyes and sat straight up. Florence Nightingale fell to the floor. Louisiana said, "I will do that right away, Granny, I promise."

"Louisiana," said Raymie.

Louisiana blinked. "Hello?" she said.

"Hi," said Raymie. "Beverly didn't show up."

"We have to go anyway," said Louisiana. She blinked again. She looked around the room. "We have to go and rescue him."

"We can't do it without Beverly," said Raymie. "We don't know how to pick locks."

All of Louisiana's bunny barrettes had migrated

to one place on her head. They had formed a gigantic clump. Something about the clump of bunny barrettes seemed sad.

"We will just have to try," said Louisiana.

There was a sudden flash of light from outside. Raymie had the ridiculous thought that Florence Nightingale had arrived carrying her great magical globe.

But it was not Florence.

It was Beverly Tapinski.

She was standing at the window. She was holding a flashlight up under her chin so that her face looked like a jack-o'-lantern.

She was smiling.

Thirty-nine

"Where were you?" said Raymie.

"Let's just say I had some things to take care of," said Beverly.

"What things?" asked Louisiana.

"I had a little sabotaging to do."

"Oh, no," said Raymie.

"It's no big deal," said Beverly. "I just threw a few trophies in the lake."

"What trophies?" said Raymie.

"Baton-twirling trophies."

"You threw Ida Nee's trophies in the lake?" said Louisiana.

"Not all of them were hers," said Beverly.

"But how could you do that?" squeaked Louisiana. "That is the end of everything. Ida Nee will call the cops again. And we will never be able to return. I will never learn how to twirl."

"Listen to me," said Beverly. "You don't need to learn how to twirl. All you have to do is sing. That will win any contest."

As soon as Beverly said the words, Raymie knew that they were true. Louisiana's singing would win any contest. And Raymie *wanted* Louisiana to win. She wanted her to become Little Miss Central Florida Tire.

Raymie stopped. She held herself very still.

"Why are you stopping?" said Louisiana.

"Come on," said Beverly. "Let's go."

Raymie started walking again.

The three of them were outside, together in the darkness, but it was surprisingly easy to see. There was Beverly's flashlight, of course. And there were streetlights and porch lights. Half a moon was hanging up in the sky, and the sidewalk in front of them glowed silver.

A dog barked.

Suddenly, the Golden Glen loomed up out of the darkness like a ship that had run aground.

"That stupid nursing home," said Beverly. "I hate that place."

"Listen," said Louisiana. She put her hand on Raymie's arm. "Shhhh."

Raymie stopped. Beverly kept walking.

"Do you hear?" said Louisiana.

Raymie heard a rustle of something in the bushes, the hum of electricity from the streetlight, the buzz of insect wings. A dog, the same one, or maybe a different one, barked and then barked again. And behind all of those noises, Raymie could hear the faint sound of music.

"Someone is playing the piano," said Louisiana.

"Whoop-de-do and so what?" said Beverly from up ahead.

It was very beautiful, sad music, which was

how Raymie knew that it was probably Chopin and that it was probably the janitor playing it. It seemed like a very long time ago that she had tried to do a good deed for Isabelle and ended up writing a letter of complaint instead. It was almost like she had been a different person then.

Raymie stared up at the Golden Glen. There was a light on in the common room.

"Come on," said Beverly. "We're wasting time."

"Isn't it the most beautiful music?" said Louisiana.

Raymie stood very still. The light from the common room lit up the top of the trees. She saw something bright yellow in the branches. Her heart thumped. She put a hand on Louisiana's shoulder.

"Look," she said.

"What?" said Louisiana. "Where?"

"Shine the flashlight up there," Raymie said to Beverly. She pointed, and Beverly shone the light up in the trees, and there was the yellow bird. He looked like the answer to everything, sitting there on a branch, tiny and perfect and winged. He cocked his head, looking down at them.

"Oh," said Louisiana. "That's the bird I rescued. That's him. Hello, Mr. Bird."

Beverly kept the flashlight trained on the yellow bird. The piano music stopped, and the bird let out a long trill of notes.

And then there was the creaking sound of a window being opened. The janitor stood and looked out into the darkness. Raymie saw his face. It was a sad face. He was looking for something.

Beverly turned off the flashlight. "Hit the ground!" she said.

All three of them lay flat on their stomachs. The sidewalk was still warm from the day's sun. Raymie leaned her cheek against it and waited. She heard Louisiana's lungs wheezing. And then the janitor whistled.

The bird stopped singing.

The janitor whistled again.

The bird whistled back.

The janitor did a more complicated whistle, and the bird answered him with a song of his own.

"Oh," said Louisiana.

And that was all any of them said. Even Beverly was silent, listening, while the janitor and the yellow bird sang to each other.

Raymie stared up at the moon. It looked like it was getting bigger, but she knew that couldn't be true. Still, the half globe of it was starting to look like something from a dream, like something that Mrs. Borkowski would have pulled out of the suitcase. And the singing yellow bird seemed like something that had been hidden in Mrs. Borkowski's dream suitcase, too.

Suddenly, Raymie was happy. It was the strangest thing, how happiness came out of nowhere and inflated your soul.

She wondered if her father was sleeping, wherever he was.

She wondered if he was dreaming of her without even really intending to do it.

She hoped so.

The whistling stopped.

The janitor said, "I know you're out there."

There was a rustling in the trees. The bird

shot up into the darkness and flew away.

"Now," whispered Beverly.

The three girls got up and ran as fast as they could.

They ran until the Golden Glen was far behind them.

When they stopped, Louisiana threw herself down on the ground. She sat on the grass with her hands on her knees and her head bent forward and worked at taking in great gulps of air.

Beverly said, "Breathe, breathe."

Louisiana looked up at them. She said, "I just love. That little. Yellow bird."

"I love him, too," said Raymie.

Louisiana smiled at her.

Beverly put the flashlight under her chin and said in a deep voice, "We all love the little bird." And then she grinned.

The world was dark. The moon was still high in the sky.

Happiness washed over Raymie again.

Forty

"Archie doesn't always do what you want him to do," said Louisiana. "Most of the time, actually, he doesn't do what you want him to do."

"What are you talking about?" said Beverly.

They were at the Tag and Bag. A shopping cart had rolled down the hill away from the store and was sitting by a tree. The silver cart was glinting merrily, reflecting the lights of the Tag and Bag parking lot.

"I'm saying that this shopping cart will be perfect to use for Archie's rescue. We can put him in it and push him and make him go wherever we want him to go."

"No," said Beverly.

"Yes," said Louisiana.

"We can't go walking around in the middle of the night with a shopping cart. It will make too much noise. Also, it will look stupid."

"I think we need it," said Louisiana. She turned to Raymie. "What do you think?"

"I guess it's okay," said Raymie. "There's no one around here anyway."

"Goody," said Louisiana. "That means we'll bring it." She pulled the cart away from the tree and started pushing it down the sidewalk.

The shopping cart had a wonky wheel that made a stuttering noise. It was as if the cart were desperate to say something, but it couldn't quite get the words out.

"Come on, you two," said Louisiana. She looked back at them. "Let's go rescue Archie." And then she turned back around and started to sing a song that was about trailers being for sale or rent.

"It's like she thinks we're in some kind of broken-down parade," Beverly said to Raymie.

They walked behind the singing Louisiana and the stuttering cart through the strange darkness. Things were visible, but everything felt insubstantial. It was almost as if gravity had less of an effect in the darkness. Objects seemed to float. Raymie felt lighter. She tried flexing her toes. They felt lighter, too.

"See that over there?" said Beverly. She pointed at the Belknap Tower. There was a light at the very top of it that blinked red. "That's where my mother works. She sits on a little stool at the register and sells miniature Belknap Towers and orange-blossom perfume and crap like that. There's a machine in the gift shop where you can put a penny into it, and the machine stretches the penny and stamps it with a picture of the tower. It's a really loud machine. My mother hates it. But then, she hates everything."

"Oh," said Raymie.

"Yeah," said Beverly.

Up ahead of them, Louisiana was still pushing the Tag and Bag cart. She was singing about being king of the road.

"Have you ever been to the top of the tower?" said Raymie.

"Lots of times," said Beverly.

"What's it like?"

"It's okay. You can see for a long way. When I was really small, I used to go up there and expect to see New York, you know? Because I was just a little kid and I didn't know any better. I would go up there and look and hope to see my dad. Which was stupid."

Raymie wondered what she could have seen from the top of the tower if she had been there at the right time. Would she have seen Mr. Staphopoulos and Edgar on their way to North Carolina? Would she have seen her father drive away with Lee Ann Dickerson?

"You can go up there with me sometime," said Beverly. "If you want."

"Okay," said Raymie.

Louisiana stopped singing. She turned to them.

"Here we are," she said.

And there it was: Building 10.

Raymie wasn't glad to see it at all.

Forty-one

If it had looked terrible in the daylight, the Very Friendly Animal Center looked even worse in the dark. The building seemed morose, and also slightly guilty, as if it had done something terrible and had hunkered itself down in the ground hoping that no one would notice.

"I bet you they don't even bother to lock the door here," said Beverly. "Who would want to get in this place anyway?"

"Us," said Louisiana. "The Three Rancheros. Hurry up. Archie is inside. He's waiting for us."

Beverly snorted. But she got out her pocket-knife and went up to the door. She said, "This won't take any time at all."

And it didn't.

She put the tip of the knife into the door-jamb and jiggled it, and a second later, the door to Building 10 swung wide. Darkness seemed to roll out of it like a cloud. It had been dark in Building 10 in the daylight. How dark would it be at night? There wasn't even the light of the single swaying bulb.

"I can't," said Raymie.

"What do you mean?" said Louisiana.

"I'll just wait here," said Raymie.

Beverly shone her flashlight into the cavern.

"Shine it on that door," said Louisiana. "I know he's behind that door."

"Yeah," said Beverly. "You said so already." She turned to Raymie. "You can wait here. It's fine."

"No," said Louisiana. "All of us. All the Rancheros. Or we don't go at all."

"Okay," said Raymie, because she had to go

where they went. She had to protect them if she could. They had to protect her.

The three of them stepped into Building 10.

Beverly's flashlight beam wavered in the darkness and then it held steady. It smelled terrible inside. Ammonia. Something rotten. Beverly shone the flashlight on the other door.

And then the horrible howl started.

Someone was dying! Someone had given up all hope! Someone was filled with a despair too terrible for words!

"Take my hand," whispered Raymie.

Forty-two

Louisiana grabbed Raymie's hand.

Raymie grabbed Beverly's hand.

The flashlight beam danced wildly around the room. It shone on the ceiling, the metal desk, the filing cabinets. It illuminated, for a moment, the single unlit bulb, and Raymie, ridiculously, felt angry at the lightbulb.

Couldn't it even try?

"Oh, my goodness, oh, no, no," said Louisiana. Her lungs wheezed. She took a deep, raspy breath and then she shouted, "Archie, here I am!"

The howling continued.

"Can you?" said Louisiana. Her teeth were chattering. "Can you unlock the other door?"

"Sure," said Beverly. They moved together, holding on to each other, toward the door. "You're going to have to let go of my hand," said Beverly to Raymie. "I need it to pick the lock."

"Okay," said Raymie. She held tight to Beverly's hand.

"Look," said Beverly, "why don't you hold the flashlight." Raymie dropped Beverly's hand and took the flashlight.

"Shine it right on the doorknob, okay?" said Beverly.

Raymie shone the flashlight on the door, just as Louisiana reached forward and turned the knob.

The door wasn't locked. It opened slowly. The sound of howling got louder.

"Archie?" said Louisiana.

Beverly took a deep breath. "Give me the flashlight," she said. She took the flashlight from Raymie and swung it around a room filled with cages. There were small cages and large cages. The small cages were piled on top of each other, and the large cages looked like human prisons, and all of the cages were empty. There wasn't a cat anywhere in sight.

It was a terrible room.

Raymie wished that she had never seen it, because now she would never forget it.

"Archie!" shouted Louisiana.

Beverly stepped farther into the room.

"They're empty," said Raymie. "No one's here."

"Who's howling, then?" said Beverly.

"Oh, Archie," whispered Louisiana. "I'm sorry."

Beverly walked around the room, swinging the flashlight in great, swirling arcs.

And then she said, "Here. Here."

Forty-three

It wasn't Archie.

It wasn't even a cat.

It was a dog. Or it might have been a dog at some point. He had ears so long that they were touching the ground. His body was small and stretched out. One eye was crusted over and swollen shut.

"Oh," said Louisiana. "He's some kind of rabbit."

"He's a dog," said Beverly.

The dog wagged his tail.

Beverly put her hand through the wire of the cage. She patted the dog on the head. "Okay," said Beverly. "Okay, it's okay." The dog wagged his tail some more. But when Beverly took her hand away, he stopped wagging his tail and started to howl.

The hair on Raymie's legs stood up. Her toes flexed without her even intending to move them.

"Right," said Beverly. "Okay." She raised the latch on the cage and opened the door. The dog stopped howling. He stepped out toward them, wagging his tail. He looked up at the three of them out of his one good eye and wagged his tail some more.

Louisiana dropped to her knees. She wrapped him up in her arms. "I'm going to call him Bunny," she said.

"That's the stupidest name I've ever heard," said Beverly.

"Let's just go," said Raymie.

Louisiana picked up the dog. Beverly shone the flashlight ahead of them, and they walked out of the terrible darkness of Building 10 and into the normal darkness of nighttime.

The moon was still up in the sky, or half of it was. It didn't seem possible to Raymie that the moon was still shining after everything that had happened. But there it was—brilliant and very far away.

Raymie sat down on the curb. Louisiana sat down next to her. The dog smelled terrible. Raymie put out her hand and touched the top of his head. There were bumps on it.

"Archie isn't dead," said Louisiana.

"Would you please shut up?" said Beverly.

"He's not dead. But he's missing and I don't know how to find him."

"Fine," said Beverly. "He's missing. Right now, what we need to do is get out of here."

"I don't think I can walk anymore," said Louisiana. "I feel too sad to walk."

"Get in the cart, then," said Beverly. "We'll push you."

"What about Bunny?" said Louisiana.

"We'll push him, too. Duh."

Louisiana stood up.

"Here," said Raymie. "Give me the dog."

Louisiana handed Bunny to Raymie, and Beverly picked Louisiana up and put her in the cart.

"It's not very comfortable in here," said Louisiana.

"Who said it would be comfortable?" said Beverly.

"No one," said Louisiana. And then she said, "I feel really sad. I feel all hollow."

"I know," said Raymie. She handed Bunny to Louisiana. Louisiana wrapped her arms around the dog.

"I wonder where Archie is," said Louisiana. "And I wonder what will become of us. Don't you wonder what will become of us?"

No one answered her.

Forty-four

Beverly was pushing the cart, and Raymie was walking beside her.

Raymie said, "I wish we could go to the top of the Belknap right now."

"Why?" said Beverly.

"Just to see if we could, I don't know, see things."

"It's dark," said Beverly. "You wouldn't see much. Besides, the place is all locked up. And you need a key to use the elevator."

"You could figure it out," said Raymie. "You could break in and find the key."

"I could break in anywhere," said Beverly. "So what? There's no point in going up there."

"Going up where?" said Louisiana.

"To the top of the Belknap Tower," said Raymie.

"Ooooh," said Louisiana. "I'm afraid of heights." She stood up in the cart and turned to face them. "I would have been a disappointment to my parents. I wouldn't have been a very good Flying Elefante."

"Yeah," said Beverly. "You said so already. Sit down before you fall over."

Louisiana sat down and gathered Bunny back into her arms.

The wonky wheel on the grocery cart stuttered and stuck as they started going uphill. Raymie and Beverly pushed together. Inside the cart, Louisiana was silent.

They were almost at the top of the hill. Raymie knew what was below them. It was Mabel Swip

Memorial Hospital, and next to that was Swip Pond, where Mrs. Sylvester went to feed the swans.

Swip Pond wasn't really a pond. Or it hadn't started out as a pond. It had started out as a sinkhole. But now it was called Swip Pond because Mabel Swip, who owned the land, had donated the sinkhole to the city and then paid for some swans and some lamps to surround it and make it look elegant.

From the top of the hill, the pond looked like a single dark eye staring at Raymie. The lamps, five of them, formed a solemn constellation of moons around the pond. There weren't any swans in sight.

Suddenly, Raymie was terribly, horribly lonely. She wished that she could find a pay phone and call Mrs. Sylvester and hear her say, "Clarke Family Insurance. How may we protect you?"

But even if she found a phone, Mrs. Sylvester wouldn't be there. It was the middle of the night. Clarke Family Insurance was closed.

Raymie tried to flex her toes.

Louisiana stood up again. She was holding Bunny close to her chest. She faced forward. "Go faster," she said.

"Are you kidding?" said Beverly. "Who do you think you are? Some kind of queen? We're pushing as hard as we can. This grocery cart is worthless. It's like the wheels aren't even wheels. It's like they're squares or something."

Raymie and Beverly pushed together.

One great push.

And somehow—how did this happen? Raymie didn't know—the cart got away from them.

They didn't let go. It wasn't that at all. It was more like the hill grabbed the cart from them. One minute, they were pushing, and the next minute, the Tag and Bag grocery cart was out of their hands, rolling down the hill.

Louisiana, Bunny in her arms, turned and looked back at Beverly and Raymie. "Oh, my goodness," she said. "Good-bye."

And then the cart and Louisiana and Bunny were gone, clattering down the hill at an impossible speed, headed right for the pond that used to be a sinkhole.

"No," said Beverly. "No."

They started to run. But the cart was done with stuttering and balking. The cart was ready to move. Even with its wonky wheel, it was faster than they were. It was determined.

From a long way away came the sound of Louisiana's voice, only it didn't sound like Louisiana. It was eerie, resigned, the voice of a ghost. And what the ghost voice said was, "But I can't swim."

Bunny started to howl his terrible end-of-the-world howl.

Raymie ran faster. She could feel her heart and soul. Her heart was beating, and her soul was right up beside her heart. No, that wasn't right. It was more like her soul was her whole body. She was nothing but soul.

And then, from somewhere in the darkness, Raymie heard Mrs. Borkowski's voice. And what Mrs. Borkowski said was, "Run, run, run."

Forty-five

Raymie ran.

Beverly ran ahead of her.

Raymie could see the grocery cart. She could see Louisiana's bunny barrettes. They were glinting, winking at her. She could see Bunny's strange, long ears blowing out behind him. They looked like wings.

And she could see a swan. He was standing at the edge of the pond. He was looking up at what was coming toward him, and he didn't look happy. Mrs. Sylvester had always said that swans were terribly moody creatures.

"Noooooo!" screamed Louisiana.

Raymie watched the Tag and Bag cart rise up in the air as if it were attempting to leave the earth altogether, and then it entered Swip Pond with a surprisingly small splash.

The swan stretched his wings out as far as they would go. He let out a noise that sounded like a complaint, or maybe it was a warning.

Beverly was at the edge of the pond now. Raymie, still running, was behind her. And this was when Raymie heard Mrs. Borkowski's voice for the last time in her life.

She did not say, "Tell me, why does the world exist?"

She did not say, "Phhhhtttt."

Mrs. Borkowski said, "You. Now. This you can do."

Raymie kept running. She ran past Beverly, who was standing and staring; she took a deep breath and dove into the pond, and the water closed over her head, and she went down as far as she could in the darkness.

She flexed her toes like Mr. Staphopoulos had taught her to do.

She opened her eyes.

She reached out her hands and parted the dark water.

Forty-six

It turned out that Bunny knew how to swim. The dog went paddling past Raymie just as she came up for air. Bunny's ears were floating on either side of his one-eyed head. He looked like a sea monster—some mythical beast, part fish and part dog.

Raymie took a deep breath and went back down under the water. She saw the Tag and Bag grocery cart. It was on its side, floating slowly toward the bottom. She reached for it. The cart was cold and heavy. And empty.

Raymie let it go. She went back up to the surface and took in another great gasp of air. She saw Beverly pulling Bunny out of the water. The swan was standing beside Beverly. He was stretching his neck and then lowering it, stretching it and lowering it, as if he were working up the courage to make an announcement.

Beverly said, "Where is she?"

Raymie didn't answer. She dove back underwater. She opened her eyes in the darkness and saw the glint of the shopping cart again. And then she saw the glimmer of a bunny barrette, a bunny barrette that was attached to the head of Louisiana Elefante.

Raymie swam toward Louisiana and pulled her into her arms.

Raymie had saved Edgar the drowning dummy from drowning many, many times. She was good at it. Mr. Staphopoulos had told her that she was good at it.

But Louisiana felt different from Edgar — she was somehow both heavier and lighter.

Raymie wrapped her arms tight around Louisiana. She kicked her feet and swam for the surface, and what Raymie thought as they rose together was that it was the easiest thing in the world to save somebody. For the first time, she understood Florence Nightingale and her lantern and the bright and shining path. She understood why Edward Option had given her the book.

For just a minute, she understood everything in the whole world.

She wished that she had been there when Clara Wingtip had drowned. She would have saved her, too.

She was Raymie Nightingale, coming to the rescue.

Forty-seven

Louisiana wasn't breathing.

And Beverly was crying, which was almost as terrifying as Louisiana not breathing.

And the swan was still trying to stretch his head right off his neck. He was leaning forward and looking at them and hissing.

Bunny was sniffing around Louisiana's head, snuffling her barrettes and letting out low moans.

Louisiana was stretched out on the grass by the pond, which was really a sinkhole. The yellow lights stood around them, looking down at them, waiting.

Raymie turned Louisiana over. She turned her head to the side. She beat on her back with her fists. Mr. Staphopoulos had taught her how to save a drowning person, how to get the water out of someone's lungs, and she did everything he had taught her to do. She remembered it all. She remembered it in the right order.

"What are you doing? What are you doing?" shouted Beverly.

Bunny moaned. The swan hissed. The yellow lights shone down.

"What are you *doing*?" asked Beverly, still crying.

Raymie pounded on Louisiana's back. A flood of water, and also a few pondweeds, exited Louisiana's mouth in a great rush. Then there was more water and more water and more water, and another weed. And then came Louisiana's squeaky, hopeful voice saying, "Oh, my goodness."

Raymie's soul was huge inside of her. She felt

a tremendous love for Louisiana Elefante and for Beverly Tapinski and for the hissing swan and the moaning dog and the dark pond and the yellow lights. Most of all, she felt love for the furry-toed and furry-backed Mr. Staphopoulos, who was gone, who had moved to North Carolina with Edgar the drowning dummy. Mr. Staphopoulos, who had put his hand on her head and told her good-bye. Mr. Staphopoulos, who had taught Raymie how to do exactly this — how to save Louisiana Elefante — before he went away.

"The hospital," said Beverly.

They picked Louisiana up together and started walking. They had gotten good at carrying her.

They went up the hill, and Bunny followed them. The swan stayed behind.

Louisiana said, "I can't swim."

"Yeah," said Beverly. "We know."

Beverly. Who was still crying.

Forty-eight

There was a nurse standing outside the hospital doors. She was smoking a cigarette. Her left elbow was cupped in her right hand, and she was holding the cigarette and staring at the four of them as they came up the hill.

"Oh, my Lord," said the nurse. She slowly lowered the cigarette. She had on a name tag that read MARCELLINE.

"She drowned," said Beverly.

"She didn't drown," said Raymie. "She almost drowned. She swallowed water."

"I have swampy lungs," said Louisiana. "I can't swim."

"Come here, baby," said Marcelline. She dropped the cigarette and took Louisiana from them and carried her through the automatic doors.

Beverly sat down on the curb. She wrapped her arms around Bunny and buried her face in his neck. "You go," she said. "I'm going to sit out here for a while."

"Okay," said Raymie. And she walked through the doors, went up to the nurse at the front desk, and asked if she could use the phone to call her mother. This nurse had a name tag that said RUTHIE. Raymie thought how nice name tags were. She wished that everyone in the world wore them.

"Look at you!" said Ruthie. "You are soaking wet."

"I was in the pond," said Raymie.

"It is five o'clock in the morning," said Ruthie. "What was you doing in a pond at five a.m.?"

"It's complicated," said Raymie. "It has to do

with a cat named Archie, who got taken to the Very Friendly Animal Center and . . ."

"And what?" said Ruthie.

Raymie tried to figure out how to explain it. She realized that she didn't even know where to begin. She was cold all of a sudden. She started to shiver.

"Have you ever heard of the Little Miss Central Florida Tire contest?" she asked.

"The what?" said Ruthie.

Raymie's teeth were chattering. Her knees were knocking together. It was so cold. "I . . ." she began again. And then, suddenly, she knew exactly what she needed to tell Ruthie. "My father ran away. He ran away with a dental hygienist named Lee Ann Dickerson, and he isn't coming back."

"That skunk," said Ruthie. She stood up and came out from behind the desk. She took off her sweater, which was a blue sweater like the one Martha at the Golden Glen wore. She draped the sweater over Raymie's shoulders.

The blue sweater smelled like roses and something deeper and sweeter even than roses. It was so warm.

Raymie started to cry.

"Shhh-shhh," said Ruthie. "Tell me your mama's phone number, and I will call her."

"Okay, yes, good morning," said Ruthie when Raymie's mother answered the phone. "Everything is just fine. I have your baby girl here at the hospital. There is nothing to worry about except that she is soaking wet because she has been swimming in a pond. Also, she told me about how her daddy run off with some woman named Lee Ann." Ruthie listened. "Mmmmm-hhhhmmm," she said after a minute. She listened some more.

"Uh-huh," said Ruthie. "Some people just skunks. There ain't no other way to say it."

Outside the glass doors, Raymie could see Beverly sitting on the curb. Her arm was around Bunny. There was lightness in the sky above their heads.

The sun was going to come up.

"You don't have to explain it to me," said Ruthie, still on the phone with Raymie's mother. "I understand all that. Yes, I do. But your baby girl is here and she is just fine and she is waiting for you."

Forty-nine

Things happened fast then. Adults showed up. Raymie's mother arrived and pulled Raymie into her arms and held her close and rocked her back and forth and back and forth. Beverly's mother showed up and sat next to Beverly on the curb, the dog in between them. And after a long while, Louisiana's grandmother arrived, too. She was wearing her fur coat, and she sat beside Louisiana's bed and held her hand and cried without making any noise at all.

Raymie told the story of what had happened again and again, how the shopping cart had gone into the water, and how Louisiana couldn't swim, and how Raymie had pulled her out of the water and pounded her on the back, and how that was something that she had learned from a man named Mr. Staphopoulos, who taught a class called Lifesaving 101.

A reporter from the *Lister Press* showed up. Raymie spelled *Elefante* for him. She spelled *Staphopoulos*. She told him that *Clarke* had an *e* on the end of it. The reporter took Raymie's picture.

And the whole time, Louisiana was asleep in a white hospital bed. She wasn't talking. She had a high fever.

But she would be fine. Everyone kept saying that she would be fine.

It was Ruthie who said, "This child needs to sleep. Everybody needs to stop asking her questions and let her go home and sleep."

But Raymie didn't want to go home. She wanted to be where Louisiana was. So Ruthie brought a cot into Louisiana's room, and Raymie lay down on it. She fell asleep right away.

And when she woke up, Louisiana was still sleeping and Louisiana's grandmother was still wearing her fur coat. She was still holding Louisiana's hand, and she was asleep, too. The hallway outside of the room was lit up, shining with afternoon light, just like the common room at the Golden Glen.

Raymie got up and stood in the doorway of the room and looked at the bright and shining path.

A cat was walking toward her.

Raymie stood and stared. The cat came closer and closer. Raymie recognized him from her dream. She recognized him from Mrs. Borkowski's suitcase.

It was Archie.

The cat brushed past her. He came into the room and leaped up on Louisiana's bed and curled himself into a tight ball.

Raymie went and lay back down on her cot. She fell asleep again. When she woke up, it was dusk and Archie was still curled up at Louisiana's feet. He was purring so loudly that the hospital bed was shaking.

Archie, King of the Cats. He had returned.

Louisiana's fever broke that night. She sat up in bed and said, "Oh, my goodness. I'm hungry." Her voice was scratchy.

And then she looked down at her feet and saw the cat.

"Archie," she said, as if she wasn't surprised at all. She bent forward and pulled him into her arms. She looked around the room. She said, "And there's Granny." She looked at her grandmother, who was sleeping in the chair beside the bed. And then Louisiana looked at Raymie and said, "Raymie Nightingale. There you are, too."

"Here I am," said Raymie.

"Where's Beverly?"

"She's at home. Taking care of Bunny."

"Bunny," said Louisiana in a voice of wonder. "We saved Bunny. Remember how we saved him?"

Ruthie came into the room and said, "How did that cat get in here?"

"He found me," said Louisiana. "I lost him. He lost me. We went looking for him, and he found me."

Raymie closed her eyes and saw Mrs. Borkowski opening the suitcase and pulling Archie out of it. "It's kind of a miracle," she said.

"Ain't no miracle," said Ruthie. "It's just a cat. That's how they do."

Fifty

The other thing that happened in the hospital was that the phone rang at the nurses' station and it was for Raymie.

Ruthie came into the room and said, "Somebody on the phone for you, Raymie Clarke."

Raymie went out into the hallway, to the phone. She still had on Ruthie's sweater. It came down to her knees.

"Hello?" said Raymie.

Ruthie was standing right beside Raymie. She put her hand on Raymie's shoulder.

"Raymie?" said the voice on the other end.

"Dad," said Raymie.

"I saw your picture. It was in the paper and . . . I wanted to check on you and make sure . . ."

Raymie couldn't think of what to say to him. She stood and held the phone up to her ear. There was nothing but a great silence. It was like listening for the ocean in a seashell and not ever hearing it.

It was like that.

After a while, Ruthie took the phone out of Raymie's hand and spoke into it. She said, "This child is tired. She has saved somebody from drowning. Do you understand what I'm saying? She saved somebody's life."

And then Ruthie hung up the phone.

"He is a skunk," she said to Raymie. "And that's all there is to it." She put her hands on Raymie's shoulders. She guided her back to Louisiana's room. Raymie got on her cot and fell back asleep.

When she woke up, she wondered if she had dreamed the whole thing.

Mostly what she remembered was holding the phone for that long silence — the silence of her father not saying anything, and her not saying anything back.

And then, too, she remembered Ruthie's hands on her shoulders, guiding her back to the room, where Louisiana was alive and breathing and a cat was curled up at her feet, sleeping.

Fifty-one

Louisiana competed in the Little Miss Central Florida Tire contest.

She wore her lucky bunny barrettes and a blue dress spangled with silver sequins. She did not twirl a baton. She sang "Raindrops Keep Fallin' on My Head."

The contest was in the Finch Auditorium. Louisiana's grandmother was there, and Beverly was there and Beverly's mother and Raymie's mother. And Raymie.

Ida Nee was there, but she did not look happy. Ruthie came from the hospital. And Mrs. Sylvester came from Jim Clarke Family Insurance. They all sat together.

Raymie's father was not there.

Raymie was not surprised — she was only happy — when Louisiana won the contest and was crowned Little Miss Central Florida Tire.

Later, after Louisiana was presented with a check for one thousand nine hundred and seventy-five dollars, and also with a sash that said LITTLE MISS CENTRAL FLORIDA TIRE 1975, Beverly Tapinski and Raymie Clarke and Louisiana Elefante went to the top of the Belknap Tower, even though Louisiana was afraid of heights.

"I'm afraid of heights," said Louisiana, who was still wearing her crown and her sash. She kept her eyes closed and lay on the floor of the observation deck.

But Raymie and Beverly stood at the railing and looked out.

"See?" said Beverly to Raymie.

"Yes," said Raymie.

"Tell me what you are seeing," said Louisiana, who was facedown on the floor and refused to stand up.

"Everything," said Raymie.

"Describe it," said Louisiana.

Raymie said, "I can see Swip Pond and the swans and Lake Clara and the hospital. I can see the Golden Glen and Jim Clarke Family Insurance. I can see Ida Nee's house and the Tag and Bag Grocery. I can see Building Ten."

"What else?" said Louisiana.

"I can see Ida Nee's moose head, and I can see the candy-corn jar on Mrs. Sylvester's desk. I can see the ghost of Clara Wingtip. I can see the yellow bird from the Golden Glen."

"Is he flying?" said Louisiana.

"Yes," said Raymie.

"What else?" said Louisiana.

"I can see Ida Nee twirling her baton. I can see Ruthie. She's waving at us. And there is Archie. And Bunny."

"Don't call him 'Bunny,'" said Beverly, who had renamed the dog Buddy.

After a while, Beverly went and picked Louisiana up and brought her to the railing.

"Open your eyes," said Beverly, "and look for yourself."

Louisiana opened her eyes. "Oh, my goodness," she said. "We're up so high."

"Don't worry," said Beverly. "I'm holding on to you."

Raymie took hold of Louisiana's hand. She said, "I've got you, too."

The three of them stood like that for a long time, looking out at the world.

Questions to Consider

1. Does the friendship of Raymie, Louisiana, and Beverly remind you of any other friendships in books or in real life?

2. What three words would you use to describe Raymie? Louisiana? Beverly?

3. Are there heroes in this story? Who do you think they are, and why?

4. A question that echoes throughout *Raymie Nightingale* is "What is life all about?" Does the story give us answers?

5. Can you relate to the girls' thoughts and fears? Do you think the kids in this story see life and death differently than the adults do?

6. Who do you think is the most hopeful character in the story? Who else is hopeful?

ONE COMMUNITY
ONE SCHOOL
ONE BOOK

When an entire community reads the same book, it becomes a point of reference for all members of that community. Conversation is sparked between booksellers and customers, librarians and patrons, teachers and students, parents and children, neighbors and friends. Reading becomes a part of that conversation. Kate DiCamillo began championing community reads initiatives across the country during her tenure as National Ambassador for Young People's Literature, and she has seen firsthand the profound impact of shared reading experiences with her own books.

For discussion guides and other resources
for Kate DiCamillo's books, please visit
WWW.KATEDICAMILLOSTORIESCONNECTUS.COM.

Join in the conversation online using #KateDiCamillo.

Follow Kate DiCamillo on Facebook at
WWW.FACEBOOK.COM/KATEDICAMILLO.

"A special treat." — *Kirkus Reviews* (starred review)

"Beautiful [and] bittersweet." — *Shelf Awareness* (starred review)

"Louisiana . . . operates with a sense of
wonder and practical optimism
(the pages shine with it)."
— *The New York Times Book Review*

Louisiana Elefante doesn't
want to leave
Raymie and Beverly,
but she seems destined
only for good-byes.

When Granny wakes her up in the middle of the
night to tell her that the day of reckoning has
arrived and they have to leave home immediately,
Louisiana isn't overly worried. After all, Granny
has many middle-of-the-night ideas. But this
time, things are different. This time, Granny
intends for them never to return.

Turn the page for an excerpt . . .

This is what happened.

We stood on the side of the road.

In Georgia.

Just past the Florida-Georgia state line. Which is not at all—in any way—a line. Yet people insist that it exists. Think about that.

Granny turned to me and said, "All will be well."

I said, "I do not believe you."

I refused to look at her.

We were both quiet for a very long time.

an excerpt from *Louisiana's Way Home*

Three semis drove past us. One was painted with a picture of a cow standing in a field of green grass. I was jealous of that cow because she was at home and I was not.

It seemed like a very sad thing to be jealous of a fake cow on the side of a truck.

I must warn you that a great deal of this story is extremely sad.

When the third semi blew past us without even slowing down, Granny said, "I am only attending to your best interests."

Well, what was in my best interests was being with Raymie Clarke and Beverly Tapinski. Raymie and Beverly were the friends of my heart, and they had been my best friends for two solid years. I could not survive without them. I couldn't. It was just not possible.

So what I said to Granny was, "I want to go home. Being with Archie is in my best interests. Raymie and Beverly and Buddy the one-eyed

an excerpt from *Louisiana's Way Home*

dog are in my best interests. You don't understand anything about my best interests."

"Now is not the time," said Granny. "This conversation is inopportune. I feel extremely unwell. But nonetheless, I am persevering. As should you."

Well, I did not care that Granny felt extremely unwell.

And I was tired of persevering.

I crossed my arms over my chest. I stared down at the ground. There were a lot of ants running around on the side of the highway looking very busy and pleased with themselves. Why would ants choose to live on the side of a highway where they were just going to get run over by cars and semis on a regular basis?

Since I was not talking to Granny, there was no one in the world for me to ask this question of.

It was a very lonely feeling.

And then an old man in a pickup truck stopped.

an excerpt from *Louisiana's Way Home*

. . .

The old man in the pickup truck was named George LaTrell.

He rolled down his window and raised his cap off his head and said, "Howdy, I am George LaTrell."

I smiled at him.

It is best to smile. That is what Granny has told me my whole life. If you have to choose between smiling and not smiling, choose smiling. It fools people for a short time. It gives you an advantage.

According to Granny.

"Now, what are you two lovely ladies doing on the side of the road?" said George LaTrell.

"Good morning, George LaTrell," said Granny. "It seems we have miscalculated and run entirely out of gasoline." She smiled a very large smile. She used all of her teeth.

"Miscalculated," said George LaTrell. "Run entirely out of gasoline. My gracious."

an excerpt from *Louisiana's Way Home*

"Could we impose upon you for a ride to the nearest gas station and back again?" said Granny.

"You could impose upon me," said George LaTrell.

I considered not imposing upon George LaTrell, because the truth is that in addition to being tired of persevering, I was also tired of imposing. Granny and I were always imposing on people. That is how we got by. We imposed. Also, we borrowed.

Sometimes we stole.

I considered not getting into the truck. I considered running down the highway, back to Florida.

But I did not think I would be able to run fast enough.

I have never been able to run fast enough.

And by that I mean that no matter where I go, Granny seems to find me.

Is that fate? Destiny? The power of Granny?

I do not know.

I got in the truck.

an excerpt from *Louisiana's Way Home*

. . .

The inside of George LaTrell's truck smelled like tobacco and vinyl. The seat was ripped up, and stuffing was coming out of it in places.

"We certainly do appreciate this, George LaTrell," said Granny.

Once somebody told Granny what their name was, she never lost a chance to use it. She said that people liked to hear the sound of their own names above and beyond any other sound in the world. She said it was a scientifically proven fact.

I doubted it very sincerely.

I sat in George LaTrell's truck and picked at the stuffing coming out of the seat, and then I threw the little pieces of stuffing fluff out the window.

"Stop that, Louisiana," said Granny.

But I didn't stop.

I threw pieces of truck stuffing out the window, and I thought about the people (and animals) I had left behind.

an excerpt from *Louisiana's Way Home*

Raymie Clarke, who loved to read and who listened to all of my stories.

Beverly Tapinski, who was afraid of nothing and who was very good at picking locks.

And then there was Archie, who was King of the Cats.

And Buddy the one-eyed dog, who was also known to us as the Dog of Our Hearts.

What if I never got the chance to use those names again?

What if I was destined to never again stand in front of those people (and that cat and that dog) and say their names out loud to them?

It was a tragic thought.

I threw more stuffing from George LaTrell's truck window. The stuffing looked like snow flying through the air. If you squinted, it did. If you squinted really hard.

I am good at squinting.

. . .

an excerpt from *Louisiana's Way Home*

George LaTrell took us to a gas station called Vic's Value. Granny started the work of talking Mr. LaTrell into pumping some gas into a can for her and also making him pay for what he pumped.

And since I had no desire to witness her efforts to get the gas that would only take me farther from my home and friends, I walked away from the two of them and went inside Vic's Value, where it smelled like motor oil and general dirt. There was a tall counter with a cash register on it.

Next to the cash register, there was a rack that was full of bags of salted peanuts, and even though my heart was broken and I was filled with the most terrible despair, my goodness, I was hungry.

I stared very hard at those little bags of peanuts.

The man behind the counter was sitting on a chair that had wheels, and when he saw me, he came out from behind the counter like a

an excerpt from *Louisiana's Way Home*

spider, moving his feet back and forth and back and forth. The chair made a squeaky exasperated noise as it rolled toward me.

"How do you do?" I said. I smiled, using all of my teeth. "My granny is outside getting some gas."

The man turned his head and looked at Granny and George LaTrell, and then he looked back at me.

"Yep," he said.

I considered him.

He had a lot of his hair in his nose.

"How much are your peanuts?" I said.

I said this even though I did not have any money at all. Granny always said, "Ask the price exactly as if you intend to pay."

The man didn't answer me.

"Are you Vic?" I said.

"Could be."

"I am Louisiana Elefante."

"Yep," he said.

He took a yellow spotted handkerchief out of

an excerpt from *Louisiana's Way Home*

his pocket and wiped it across his forehead. His hands were almost entirely black with grease.

I said, "I have been made to leave home against my will."

"That right there is the story of the world," said Vic.

"It is?" I said.

"Yep."

"I hate it," I said. "I have friends at home."

Vic nodded. He folded his spotted handkerchief up into a neat square and put it back in his pocket.

"You can take as many of them little bags of peanuts as you want to," he said. He nodded in the direction of the peanut rack.

"Free of charge," he said. And then he rolled himself back around the counter.

Well, this was the only good thing that had happened to me since Granny woke me up at three a.m. and told me that the day of reckoning had arrived.

In some ways, this is a story of woe and

an excerpt from *Louisiana's Way Home*

confusion, but it is also a story of joy and kindness and free peanuts.

"Thank you," I said.

I helped myself to fourteen bags.

Vic smiled at me the whole time I was taking the peanuts from the rack.

There is goodness in many hearts.

In most hearts.

In some hearts.

I love peanuts.

an excerpt from *Louisiana's Way Home*

Beverly Tapinski has run away
from home plenty of times.
This time, it's not running away.
It's leaving.

A New York Times Bestseller

★ "Deeply meaningful." — *Publishers Weekly* (starred review)

★ "DiCamillo writes in a spare style, describing small, seemingly
disparate moments that gradually come together in a rich,
dynamic picture. The other thing she does brilliantly is shape
characters whose eccentricities make them heartbreakingly,
vividly real." — *Booklist* (starred review)